Dr Mehmood Syed is an alumnus of the Guy's, King's, and St. Thomas' School of Medicine at King's College London and a Consultant in Family Medicine. He holds the Diploma of the Royal College of Obstetricians and Gynaecologists, Membership of the Royal College of General Practitioners, and an MBA from the Business School of Imperial College London. He is the author of several academic papers and co-author of an internationally published textbook of primary care.

After practising medicine for a decade in London, Mehmood transitioned first into healthcare management and then general business management in the Middle East. He presently resides in Dubai with his wife, their two children, and three cats.

For Nairah, Da'oud and Laila. May you always know love and happiness.

Mehmood Syed

Empire of the Sun God

Austin Macauley Publishers

LONDON • CAMBRIDGE • NEW YORK • SHARJAH

Copyright © Mehmood Syed 2022

The right of Mehmood Syed to be identified as author of this work has been asserted by the author in accordance with Federal Law No. (7) of U.A.E., Year 2002, Concerning Copyrights and Neighboring Rights.

All rights reserved. No part of this publication may be reproduced, stored in a retrieval system, or transmitted in any form or by any means, electronic, mechanical, photocopying, recording, or otherwise, without the prior permission of the publishers.

Any person who commits any unauthorized act in relation to this publication may be liable to legal prosecution and civil claims for damages.

The age group that matches the content of the books has been classified according to the age classification system issued by the Ministry of Culture and Youth.

ISBN – 9789948046691 – (Paperback)
ISBN – 9789948046707 – (E-Book)

Application Number: MC-10-01-7169459
Age Classification: E

Printer Name: iPrint Global Ltd
Printer Address: Witchford, England

First Published 2022
AUSTIN MACAULEY PUBLISHERS FZE
Sharjah Publishing City
P O Box [519201]
Sharjah, U.A.E.
www.austinmacauley.ae
+971 655 95 202

Every thought, every decision, and every action are the inevitable consequence of a nexus of uncountable preceding events stretching back from the present moment to the birth of time.

If, therefore, I have made some small achievement or had some positive impact on the lives of others, then for them all, the credit is due to Allah. Truly, only the mistakes have been mine.

Prologue

Ten Carthagian-days prior to his death, Duke Ichiro Hazahari donned the uncomfortable straps of a harness around his legs and buttocks and clipped himself to the long metal cable of the winch that would lower him to the cavern his miners had discovered. Dr Andrea Martin was one of only a few academics on Carthage and accompanied him into the cave below. A professor of economics on Earth, she now taught undergraduate economics at the colony's only university. But she had studied archaeology as an undergraduate herself in London, and for this reason, the Duke had sent Dr Martin images taken of the cavern. Before providing her opinion however, she wanted to see the cave for herself. The Duke wanted the same, confident he would reveal the hoax it clearly was. Some mischievous attempt at humour from his miners, he had no doubt, which, to the Duke's annoyance, was causing a suspension of mining activity in the quarry, and which would endanger his ability to meet his trade commitments.

The quarry where the cave had been discovered was fifty miles north of the principal city of his desert planet. A large plasma drill had been used to cut through rock towards, what had looked like, a large lithium ore deposit on subterranean imaging scans. However, after three hundred or so metres of slow drilling, the plasma beam had punctured a cavity in the rock and immediately shut down in response; an automated safety feature designed to prevent ignition of flammable gases that might be trapped in the rock. The miners had flown a camera into the cavern to take look at what they had found and promptly alerted the Duke's office to the discovery.

Dr Martin had been lowered first into the cave. The drill shaft was about a metre in diameter, its walls smooth to the touch of her gloved hands but scorched black by the heat of the plasma beam that had burned through the red-brown rock. As she was lowered into the cave, the beam of the lamp on her bright yellow hard-hat cast a white oval which searched over the cave floor and walls as she turned her head to take in the view.

The cavern was large, approximately ten metres across with ancient stalactites hanging from the ceiling, and red-brown boulders strewn across the uneven floor. The stalactites suggested water had once dripped from the cave ceiling, but if there had ever been water on this barren planet, there was none now, save for that imported by the Duke on a monthly basis. What had caught the miners' attention and what gave Dr Martin pause, was a large cairn in the approximate centre of the cave. It was almost a metre high and two metres long and was composed of numerous red brown rocks which looked as if they had been taken from around the cave. The rough, uneven ceiling was approximately three metres above the cavern floor, from which the winch stopped a metre short, forcing the academic to unfasten herself and drop the remaining distance, which she managed with ease. On the opposite side of the cave she could see a large boulder of smooth, black rock amidst a pile of rocks, and above them, signs of scorching. Otherwise, the cave was filled only with rocks and boulders of the same red-brown shade as the sand that covered the planet. The Duke was soon alongside her as she examined the cave, recording a video of her exploration with a small handheld camera.

The cairn was topped by a large, roughly rectangular slab of smooth, red-brown rock with strange markings in three distinct columns, of which the Duke could make no sense. "What do you make of this?" he asked.

"I was curious about that when I saw the pictures. I did a little research, and it appears the markings are cuneiform. It's the earliest form of writing ever discovered on Earth and dates to Mesopotamia from between four thousand B.C. to around one hundred A.D."

"This makes no sense. How can this be here?"

"It's very strange. This is obviously not a natural rock fall, someone, or something, has clearly been buried here. But *cuneiform*…a billion miles from Earth…that's something else. But…I mean if…if this is for real, it would rewrite everything we think we understand about human history. But if it's a hoax, what would be the point?"

"I think we'll find the answer to that under these rocks." The Duke bent to slide the slab off the cairn.

"I wouldn't. We don't know anything about this yet, let's not go tampering with it just yet – just in case this is for real."

"Okay…sure," he reluctantly paused, then left the rock slab in place and straightened up. "Can you read the inscription?"

"I can't, I'm afraid. I don't know enough about cuneiform to make a meaningful translation. We also don't know what language it's written in. I have sent the images to an academic I used to know in London who's now on Vega-3, to see if she can make sense of it. I'm waiting to hear back from her."

"You don't know what language it's in?"

"Sorry, I didn't explain. Cuneiform is not a language per say, it's a writing system that depicts sounds. In theory, it could be used to codify almost any language, so first we need to convert the markings into sounds and then hope the sounds are intelligible as some known language. If they're not, then we're a little stuck."

"I see, I had no idea. But if it was written in a known language, why wouldn't someone simply write in that language, why use cuneiform?"

Dr Martin shrugged. "No idea."

"Okay, let's say this room dates back to one hundred A.D. or earlier. Obviously, there is no way that humans could have placed this here."

"So…we're talking, what…aliens?" she said with a chuckle.

"Well, let's not get ahead of ourselves. If we say humans from one hundred A.D. or earlier couldn't have placed it here and, as there is no evidence of aliens, then clearly it doesn't date from one hundred A.D., and it must therefore be a hoax by someone on this colony. That lump of black rock there looks like someone has drilled down here before, but not drained the molten rock whilst drilling. But, then who in this colony would know anything about cuneiform writing?" The Duke was silent for a moment as he pondered his own question. "I'll have the miners interviewed, to see if anyone is hiding anything. I just don't believe anyone from our colony would have done this. Which must mean someone else put this here, but if so, then who? And why?"

"I believe there is an archaeology professor on Hydrax Prime, I don't remember his name. Perhaps you could reach out to them and get their assistance? I think we might be able to find some way to date the cairn, which would probably tell us whether this a hoax or not."

The thought of seeking help from Hydrax Prime was distasteful to the Duke. He had no love for the Emperor, who made his seat of power there, or his policies of control. But then again, perhaps reaching out to the Emperor for assistance was just what he needed to reassure him of his loyalty whilst his own embryonic opposition to Imperial rule, slowly took shape.

The Duke soon radioed up to the surface and was winched to the top. He gave instructions that no further excavation of the quarry should occur and that no-one should be allowed entry to the cave below without his leave.

Late in the night, the Duke sat in his tower office and composed an email to the Emperor's office, summarizing what had been found and attaching pictures taken of the cavern, the cairn, and the inscribed slab. He requested dispatch of a research team suitably equipped to document and examine the cavern.

After sending the message, he rose from his desk and stepped out onto his high balcony and into the warm night air. The blackness of the night was illuminated by the familiar river of stars that hung across the dome of the sky from north to south. There was no moon this night and the billions of stars before him were unabashed in their radiance of whites, yellows, and pale blues. In their midst, the great red star of the

Hydraxian system stared down at him like the angry eye of some giant beast, studying his duplicity and weighing his crimes. He felt its malevolence and wondered how long it would be before his alliance would emerge from the shadows, and the inevitable confrontation with the Emperor would then begin.

Unbeknown to the Duke however, the Emperor was already aware of his archaeological discovery as well as the Duke's planned alliance of the colonies and was sending his envoy to meet with the Duke.

Chapter 1

Red flame streaked across the azure sky, tearing at the Duke's serenity like a knife across his skin. With his binoculars, Duke Hazahari could see the Imperial shuttle at the head of the flame; its dark underbelly glowing red as it made its descent through the Carthagian atmosphere. Three days and a long night he had spent pondering the purpose of the envoy's visit and, he wondered still what events this omen might portend.

The Duke quickly moved into his air-conditioned office to collect an earpiece from his desk. Cool air washed over him like surf, providing welcome respite from the incessant heat that beat down on his dry, barren planet. Bookcases lined two of the walls his small triangular office and every space within them was jammed to bursting with thick texts on quantum mechanics, quantum gravity, information theory and other obscure physics subjects. His broad brown desk stood opposite the glass door to his balcony, but the brown of the desktop was barely visible beneath the pile of maps and printouts that had accumulated in recent days. From across the back of the desk, he shoved the documents aside, rooting for one of his small black earpieces and, finding one, placed it in his ear, tapping it as he did so, to speak with his personal synthetic intelligence. "Cyrus, why are you bringing the

Imperial shuttle in at such great speed? Slow it down before it burns up and take it to the Eastern Landing Zone. I will make my way there to meet them."

"I'm afraid, sir, the Imperial craft is not under my control. They have insisted on landing in the central square and have refused automated guidance. I have attempted to dissuade them from landing in the square, but it appears they require an audience with you urgently. I have therefore summoned police to clear the square."

What does this mean? the Duke thought to himself. He searched through the possibilities. *Could the Emperor know of my plans? If so, how? Could someone have betrayed me?* he wondered. "Tell no-one of this meeting, the Emperor has spies everywhere," the Duchess Aisha had warned, and he had not. Not even his wife knew of his planned alliance. "Cyrus, Hydrax Prime were supposed to send a research team but instead they are sending Alexion herself to meet with me. Now she is blazing across the sky in a hurry to land right on my doorstep. What is going on? Any thoughts?"

"I'm afraid, sir, there is insufficient information at this time to formulate a cogent hypothesis."

Cyrus' familiar reply in the face of uncertainty, irritated the Duke now, more than ever. *Twenty million New Dollars for a quantum synthetic intelligence and this is the best it can do?* The Duke pulled off his earpiece and flicked it back into the confusion of papers on his desk, before stomping around it to slump heavily into the desk's black leather chair. He opened a locked draw to his right, shuffled some more papers out of the way and withdrew a matt black plasma handgun with a wide oval barrel. He turned it over in his hands, then powered it on. Feeling a small measure of reassurance as the lights on the handle illuminated in sequence to indicate the level of destructive power it held.

After a few moments, he rose once again, tucked the weapon into the waistband of his trousers, and returned to the balcony to look again upon his visitors. The Imperial shuttle continued on its approach to the surface, seemingly undamaged by its hurried descent. If it were to suddenly explode into flame, he would not be disappointed, but it was clear such fortune would not smile upon him today. Short triangular wings opened from beneath the fuselage of the vessel, round jets swivelling upright within the wings and firing to control its dive down towards him.

Looking off to the east, the Duke could see the dark rocky peaks of the Kirishima mountain range which lined the eastern and southern fringes of the plateau upon which his small colony was built. The mountains formed jagged black teeth which reached up several hundred metres, as if to bite at the dome of the cloudless sky above but looked much more sinister than their namesake he remembered from his youth. Beyond them he knew persistent storms of sand and flint would be raging and he was grateful for the protection the mountainous wall accorded to his small colony. In the distance to the west, the quarry managed by the *Imperial Mining Corporation* was busy with heavy droids moving and sifting rocks, ever in search of the lithium, gold and uranium that was his colony's wealth by rights and for which the Imperium compensated him in water. His own quarry to the north was idle since the discovery of the mysterious cairn there, three hundred metres below the surface, the meaning of which he was yet to fully comprehend.

In the city's central square, below the Duke's balcony, he could see his son sparring with his Master of Arms. The clunking of their wooden training swords was faintly audible even from the height of the Duke's balcony as the two men clashed and parried. A small crop of young women watched the men nearby and the Duke immediately understood why they had elected to train outside the residence's tall perimeter wall.

Across the square, opposite the ducal residence, the midday *adhan* began to boom from the city's Grand Mosque. Its melodic Arabic rising and falling, calling the faithful to prayer by exalting the greatness of the god the Duke had no faith in, but to which his wife was ever devoted. Groups of the faithful began making their way across the cobblestone square to assemble before the new metal detectors erected at the main entrance. Leaving them to their prayers, the Duke returned once more to his office to ponder.

Below, Nobuhide Watanabe, the Duke's thirty-eight year old Master of Arms paused his attack on the Duke's son, Ibrahim, and cocked his head towards the Grand Mosque. "Shouldn't you be running along?" he said as he pulled off his heavy helmet with its oval grille of horizontal metal bars and thick padding to protect his neck and shoulders. His face was slender and stubbled with a sharp nose and swift brown eyes that rarely missed his opponents' moves.

"Forget it, I'm not in the mood today," Ibrahim replied, pulling off his helmet and mussing his flattened hair, slick with sweat, to let it fall in black wavy curls almost to his shoulders.

"Oh okay, its optional now, I get it. But don't get me wrong five times a day, every day, would be a pain for anyone."

"It's always been optional, it's not that. I'm just not feeling it these days. To be honest, I'm not sure if I ever really believed it. All that bowing and praying to a god who, if he does exist, obviously isn't interested…I'm not sure it's for me."

"Because of the attack?"

"Maybe," he replied with a sigh. The memory of the recent brutality Ibrahim had witnessed was seldom far from his thoughts, now. "I mean there were kids there. They got ripped apart…and the sound…of men screaming…I don't think I will ever forget that."

"I know, it's hard, my friend, but your dad's doing everything he can to hunt these bastards down. We'll get them…soon, and then we'll make them pay. Why don't you talk to the imam, maybe he can help?"

Ibrahim was far away now thinking of the attack. "They think they may have gone off-world, you know, maybe to Alsuwayra. There was an unscheduled shuttle launch about an hour afterwards and apparently it headed in that direction."

"I know, but the Alsuwayreans have always been good to us. I doubt they had anything to do with it."

"Who knows...things are messed up these days." Replacing his helmet, he jokingly changed the subject, "Now, you going to try to hit me or what, old man!"

"Old man hey? Oh! We'll see!" Nobuhide lunged forward bringing his training sword down at the helmet of his opponent, but Ibrahim was a beat faster and parried the blow with his sword, pushing the older man back a step and following with a blow to his opponent's chest of his own, making a loud thwacking noise as it struck his metal breastplate.

The roar of the shuttle's jets reverberated through the streets of the small city, as the grey and black vessel descended in diminishing spirals around the white-washed brick buildings bordering the square, drawing ever closer with each circuit. Several people began taking photos of it with their camera phones and Ibrahim and Nobuhide also interrupted their training to watch the vessel from a nearby bench as its roaring jets grew louder. The Imperial insignia of two crossed swords behind an upright clenched fist, was emblazoned in gold on the charred underbelly of the vessel. The cockpit, angled downwards from the main fuselage, made the vessel look like some enormous predatory animal poised to pounce on some unseen prey.

Two white police cars arrived at the far side of the square with bright blue and red sirens flashing and three officers in dark blue uniforms, began clearing people to make way for the shuttle. One of the officers started to approach Ibrahim and Nobuhide, but on recognizing the Duke's son, abruptly turned away and occupied himself instead with the lay people still staring up at the shuttle. Once the people had been cleared to its periphery, the shuttle began hovering over the central area of the square, its wing-jets charring the stone cobbles beneath as they kicked up large plumes of red-brown sand and dust, further encouraging the onlookers to scatter. The shuttle hung there for a long moment before landing props eventually lowered from its fuselage and wings, and the vessel touched down gently.

As soon as the vessel touched stone, the jets began powering down and the undercarriage of the fuselage opened with a loud hiss, descending to the ground to form a dark ramp. At the top of it stood a slender blonde-haired woman, wrapped in a burgundy and gold silk dress that fell to her knees. She had an attractive oval face, fixed with a stern, determined expression, and piercing blue eyes. As the dust settled, she glided elegantly down the ramp into the harsh midday glare but was followed closely behind by two bulky military droids, their heavy metal feet thudding loudly as they stomped behind their master.

Ibrahim and Nobuhide watched the droids with growing alarm. Each droid was approximately six feet tall and half as wide at the shoulder. They appeared to have been chiselled from two huge blocks of black steel with muscled black plating over their chests and lobstered grey metal plates over their necks and abdomens. Their heads were black cuboids with sharp angular edges which narrowed together into a point at the back of the head. Their eyes the colour of fresh blood, above a mesh grating where their mouths should be and over the left breast of each, blazed the Imperial insignia debossed in gold. Arising from the right forearm of each droid, the wide barrel of a black plasma rifle had been unfolded, in apparent readiness for battle. The party of three approached the main gate of the ducal residence and as they did so, the gates slid apart to allow the visitors entry. Ibrahim nodded to Nobuhide, and the pair donned their helmets and discretely followed the droids at a distance, the tall gate locking back into place with a clang, as they passed.

As the three visitors made their way towards the imposing black doors of the white stucco-fronted residence, one of the military droids stopped abruptly and turned to challenge the followers they had acquired. Drawing its right arm to point its weapon at the two men, the droid commanded in a low tone. "Halt! State your business here."

"I am Ibrahim Hazahari, son of Duke Hazahari. It is you who should state your business to me!" he replied boldly, pulling off his helmet to show his face as Nobuhide's instinct immediately moved his hand to the hilt of his wooden sword.

At the droid's deep metallic growl, the woman ahead stopped and turned to the two Carthagians. She looked them up and down from a distance and closely inspected their wooden training swords as well as their traditional blue and brown kendogu armour. A small square of white light circled the periphery of both her blue eyes for a moment, and without a word, she turned to resume her walk to the main entrance of the residence. The droid facing Ibrahim immediately lowered its arm and turned away.

Inside his office, Duke Hazahari prepared for his meeting. He moved his handgun to the waistband at his back and donned a black blazer to match his trousers, hoping it would be enough to hide the bulky weapon. On his way to the door, he stopped at a low cupboard, upon which his late father's katana was displayed on an ebony stand in its ornately engraved silver scabbard. He paused for a moment, then collected the katana and made his way out.

As he sped down the spiral staircase that lined the tower of his office and descended to the main building below, he once again considered the possible motives for this visit. He had met Alexion, the rendering of the Emperor's synthetic intelligence, on only one occasion previously but it was unusual for the sentient system to synchronise into a droid at all, let alone use it to make visits to the colonies. He knew something crucial was happening, but he wasn't sure quite how alarmed he should be. *If one of the other colonies has talked, we're all dead,* he thought. The Duke exited the stairwell of his tower and entered a small antechamber. A door to his right would open to a staircase leading directly into the reception room whilst the door to his left would lead to the private chambers of his residence, from where a further staircase would allow him to enter the reception area on its far side, offering him a brief opportunity to spy his visitor from a distance. He chose the door on his left which opened onto a corridor running alongside the bedrooms of his home. Behind a closed door to his left he could hear the thumping of his wife's feet as she ran on a treadmill with the low rhythmic thumping of music playing in the room. He moved to open the door but paused with his hand on the door handle, then turned away. Deciding instead to continue on his way without alarming his wife. *It's too late to explain now*, he thought.

At the end of the corridor the grey-veined white marble flooring gave way to a staircase curving away to the right with an ornate cast iron balustrade on its right side. He swept quickly down the stairs and into the main reception area of the residence at its far side, still slightly breathless from his swift descent from his tower office. The reception room was rectangular with high ceilings and a tall arch midway along its length on the Duke's left, opening into the main entrance foyer and the doors to the central square beyond. Alexion was already seated facing the Duke on a leather armchair, near the centre of the room, with a long settee to her right and a matching armchair directly across from her on the opposite side of a low rectangular glass coffee table. At the arch to the entrance foyer the Duke saw the two military droids for the first time. They were standing motionless like steel statues, at each foot of the arch, facing into the room, and behind them his son and Nobuhide stood by the front door to the residence. He glimpsed the barrels of plasma rifles drawn from the droids' forearms and immediately felt the icy jaws of a vice clench across his chest. Beads of sweat began to gather on his brow as his heart pounded ferociously.

Trying his best to breathe easily and suppress his racing thoughts, he slowly approached the Alexion droid, which rose as he did so. He greeted her as warmly as he could muster, shaking her metal hand, covered in fake flesh, which for a droid, was oddly warm to the touch. He swallowed hard and discretely wiped his brow in a casual gesture, hoping his anxiety would go unnoticed. "Alexion, it is always a pleasure. Welcome to our humble colony. I see you have already met my son." Turning now to Ibrahim, he instructed, "Son, why don't you and Nobuhide go upstairs, I believe your mother is looking for you."

"I'm sure he is just fine where he is," Alexion replied coldly, inspecting the katana in the Duke's left hand as Ibrahim shook his head discretely in refusal. The Duke placed the katana on the settee to his left with the handle within his reach and sat at the edge of the armchair opposite the Imperial envoy, conscious of the bulky weapon at his back. "Duke, may I ask the purpose of this sword?" she said as she retook her seat and casually crossed her legs at the knee to reveal the smooth false skin of her carefully sculpted legs.

"It's nothing, I was on my way to polish it that is all. But in turn may I ask you of the purpose of your droids? I understood you were coming to see the cavern we found."

"Your mysterious cavern will have to wait I'm afraid. Our scientists are somewhat occupied at the moment. We will send a research crew in time, but the droids are…necessary."

The Duke was alarmed at the envoy's comment, the Emperor was clearly not interested what could be the most significant archaeological discovery in history, which meant there could only be one other reason for this impromptu visit and that could only mean death for him and his family. Before the Duke could respond, the envoy continued, "As you know of course, the Emperor is very interested in the wellbeing of all the colonies he maintains, not least of which is Carthage as an important source of lithium for all the Empire. The Emperor has recently become aware of a threat from amongst the colonies which disturbs the peaceful equilibrium he has established in the trade for water from Hydrax Prime. The Emperor is concerned about efforts to sabotage this trade and I have come to learn of what you know of this threat."

The Duke gripped the armrest of his chair and forced himself not to bolt from the room. *She knows something. She must know of the meeting, but no-one would have talked. She clearly doesn't know everything, otherwise I would have been arrested already. But then why is she here in person, with her droids?* The Duke took a deep breath and tried to calm himself. "I'm afraid Alexion, you needn't have troubled yourself by coming here, a simple call would have been sufficient. I'm afraid I don't know of any threat to the Emperor. Of course we have suffered a terrorist attack recently by some fanatics, but we are still investigating that incident and trying to identify the culprits. Is that what you are referring to?" *Stick to the lie, there is no way to bargain out of this*, he thought.

"Duke, we know you had a meeting with several other colonies recently on Alsuwayra Ithnayn. We want to know which other colonies are involved in this rebellion and what your plans are." Her synthetic face betrayed an expression of boredom on her artificial face, which could only have been deliberate.

Rebellion, he thought. He knew was in grave danger now and felt the beads of cold sweat forming again on his brow. "My dear Alexion, I'm afraid you are mistaken. There is no *rebellion*, certainly not from Carthage. Yes, indeed there was a meeting of several colonies on Alsuwayra, but this was in response to the terrorist attacks here and on that planet to discuss what had happened and try to cooperate to retaliate against the group responsible. That is all. We are always grateful for the Emperor's goodwill to this planet and his fair distribution of water to all the colonies. There is no plan to disrupt or disturb that…err…balance." *In for a penny, in for a pound*, he thought as he compounded his lie.

"Duke, as you well know, the meeting occurred three Earth-days *before* the attack on your mosque. We know the meeting was held specifically to try to draw the planets into some sort of misguided alliance to challenge the Emperor's authority and I'm afraid your pitiful attempt at deceit and your underhanded rebellion will not be tolerated." The droid stood once again. "I will be relieving you of your command of this colony with immediate effect. You will be taken into custody back to Hydrax Prime where you will be questioned further about this matter…unless of course you are willing to share the names of the others involved in this plot?"

Duke Hazahari wiped at his brow with the palm of his hand, then gripped the bridge of his nose between his thumb and forefinger. He closed his eyes for a moment as he took another deep breath. He knew interrogation would undoubtedly mean pain and death. He looked across at his son and in that moment, he remembered a simpler time on Earth. Before the war. Before the air and seas were poisoned. When Ibrahim was still a child. Munching ice cream happily in their small London garden. His hair, an untidy mop of black curls. His little legs, not yet able to reach the ground from his chair. Alexion watched the Duke and his sword closely, expecting him to reach for it at any moment – just as the Duke had intended. He took another deep breath and knew he had no choice but to plunge.

In one swift movement he stood from his chair, reached for the gun at his back, and fired at the Imperial envoy. A long ribbon of orange plasma flew from the gun, crackling with electrical charge as it did so. The beam whipped forwards and struck Alexion squarely in the chest, throwing her backwards to the floor, igniting her clothing, and leaving a gaping hole in her chest. But before Alexion's body had hit the floor, the military droids had fired. Plasma beams shot across the room blasting the settee to the Duke's left which exploded in a cloud of duck feathers and flame, as another blast struck the Duke, tearing across his chest and hurling him to the ground behind the now burning settee.

As the droids began to fire, Ibrahim and Nobuhide leapt forwards. They drew their training swords and fell upon the droids closest to each of them. Nobuhide struck his opponent repeatedly with his sword aiming for the head of the droid. In a brief moment of its disorientation, he succeeded in pushing the droid sufficiently for it to fall to its side, crashing against a sideboard in the foyer. The sideboard collapsed under the weight of the droid and a large mirror hanging above it crashed and splintered to the ground. As the droid writhed on the floor in an effort to stand, Nobuhide drove the pointed end of his wooden sword upwards between broken seams in its metal armour at its neck, destroying whatever processors were held in his head, and bringing its thrashing to an end.

Ibrahim was also aiming for the head of the droid closest to him. With all his strength he smashed and smashed at the droid, but with little effect. The droid attempted to push him off and to bring its right arm to fire at the youth, but Ibrahim hit its arm away, sending a plasma blast across the main reception room, obliterating a bookcase on its far side to leave long trailing scorch marks across the milky white marble wall, like black veins on skin. For a moment, the whine of the plasma weapons and the smell of burning furniture and flesh, brought Ibrahim back to the recent horror of the mosque attack. Never had Ibrahim felt more powerless, as he cowered behind a wide pillar of the mosque watching the mass murder unfold. But now in this moment, he was determined not to let his attackers succeed.

Duchess Mariam stopped her treadmill. The crashing of furniture and the high whine of plasma blasts were unmistakable. She hopped off the machine and ran straight to a door leading from her private gymnasium into her bedroom. She darted to her wardrobe and dropped to her knees, pausing for a moment at an ebony box with a gold clasp, on the floor of her wardrobe. Ignoring the box, she rifled through a small pile of clothes that had fallen to the wardrobe floor, until she found what she was looking for. She pulled out a plasma handgun, similar to that her husband kept in his desk, and hastily powered it on, whilst moving across to the bedroom door and kicking off her trainers, to move silently in her socks. She opened the bedroom door cautiously, bending low with the gun ready. The upstairs hall was clear and without hesitation, she ran swiftly to the curved marble staircase that led down to the main reception area from where the sound of crashing furniture and plasma discharges continued to emanate.

Ducking low behind the balustrade of the staircase she looked out from gaps in its floral design and gasped at the shocking scene before her. Her son was struggling with one of the military droids as its plasma beams whipped randomly across the room destroying everything they touched. Nobuhide was injured, caught by a plasma blast, he was sat leaning against a fallen droid in the entrance foyer, cradling his left arm across his chest as he attempted to stand. In the middle of the room she could see her husband lying motionless in a pool of blood which was spreading slowly across the white marble floor. Near him the fallen Alexion droid was lying on her back, immobile, but sparking from the hole in her chest, her clothes smouldering. Much of the furniture in the room was destroyed or on fire and the white stone walls were scorched. The smell of ionised air and burning filled the room.

The Duchess moved silently down the steps, staying low behind the ornate balustrade until she had no choice but to emerge into plain sight. As she did so, she quickly ducked behind a toppled bookcase and swiftly made her way over the remains of her furniture towards the arch of the entrance foyer and her son.

Ibrahim was losing his grip now. He had lost his training sword and had grabbed the droid's right arm with both hands as it flung him from side to side against the wall, all the while firing plasma across the room as it attempted to shake the boy's grip. When she was close enough to fire accurately without being hit by the droid's plasma beams, the Duchess jumped up from behind an overturned table near the archway and drew the gun out in front of her with both hands on the grip. She shouted to her son to get down, and shot at the droid, decapitating it slowly with a single prolonged orange blast.

As the droid and its head crashed to the floor with heavy thuds, the Duchess satisfied herself that the other droids were destroyed and that her son was safe, then quickly rushed to her husband's aid and began pressing on his wound with a nearby pillow. Police from the square were rushing into the residence now with their weapons drawn, summoned by Cyrus, as he watched from the residence's security systems. She quickly instructed the officers to call an ambulance – but only for Nobuhide; the Duke was already dead.

Chapter 2

As Duke Hazahari lay dying on the floor of his home, Alistair Jamieson stood before the Great Pyramid on Hydrax Prime, grasping a small tablet computer in his left hand and feeling the weight of the pyramid as it stared down at him. The pyramid reached a full kilometre into the blue-green sky above and was clad in sheets of polished gold that shone so brightly in the red light of the Hydraxian sun that he had to shield his eyes from their glare. He had heard rumours that the pyramid extended for almost a kilometre below ground as well, and that access to those lower levels was securely guarded. He could only wonder what secrets might lay buried there.

The golden walls of the pyramid were perfectly smooth and unbroken except, for two tree-lined terraces that jutted out from its sides just below the apex and were, more often than not, wrapped in a shroud of white cloud. The Throne Room was on that level some four hundred floors up and elevators inside would soon whisk him up to that grand hall.

Alistair stood almost five hundred metres away at the foot of a long grey stone walkway that was lined on either side by tall palm trees. The walkway stretched in a perfectly straight line from where he stood, to the pyramid's enormous twin ebony doors that were each gilded with the Emperor's insignia. He could hear surf lapping against the stone shoreline of the bay to his back and smell the salt of the vast ocean beyond, in the air. Away in the west he could see a shaft of bright white sunlight cast down from the sky by enormous geostationary lenses in orbit, boiling the ocean to produce the limitless clean energy required to power the vast population of drones that served the Emperor. In the east and north the vast emerald forests of the Imperial estate stretched as far as his eyes would allow him to see and were composed of giant ancient redwood and cedar trees that were easily three hundred feet tall with trunks almost ten feet wide.

Alistair counted seven heavy black droids standing motionless around the base of the pyramid, watching for potential threats with their ghostly red eyes. There would be more hidden around the pyramid, he knew, but the less threatening slender white droids were the denizens of the pyramid itself. Each of them was a few inches shorter than their black brothers with a lightweight frame, slender arms and legs and pale blue eyes. Unlike the black droids, they carried no obvious weapons and acted as the servants of the pyramid, fetching, carrying, and doing the Emperor's bidding whenever required. To Alistair though, their main task seemed to be herding the swarms of people who sought audience with the Emperor's Envoy one level below the Throne Room or who arrived daily to offer prayers to the self-styled Sun-God himself.

Gathering his wits together and taking a deep breath, Alistair began making his way up the stone walkway to present his report. He was a large man, standing almost six feet tall with a heavy muscular build and intimidating to behold to most of the subordinates who worked for him as the Chief Executive of the Imperial Mining Corporation. The hair on his head had mostly relocated to his arms and other than thin red patches over his ears and the back of his head, he was completely bald with a scattering of freckles in place of the thick red hair he had known in his youth. His large arms however, which were thick with red hair over freckled pale skin but were now hidden beneath a rich white cotton shirt and dark blue silk and wool jacket that matched his trousers. His thick neck was chafed by the unaccustomed formality of the buttoned collar and silk tie he wore beneath the jacket, but he ignored the scratching at his neck, and continued on his march towards the Emperor.

Alistair had been with the Imperial Mining Corporation for the last seven Earth-years, rising quickly within its ranks to become its Chief Executive, following the success of his bold proof of concept, four Earth-years ago. He had obtained black market plasma rifles on Vega-3 and publicly demonstrated their superiority to the traditional steels and bits that his obsequious predecessors had insisted on using for drilling. Since then plasma mining had become the de facto standard across all the colonies and the Imperium had taken note, elevating the son of a failed used-car dealer, to the highest seat in one of the most powerful organisations, in the new Empire.

As he made his way towards the pyramid's imposing doors, he thought over the mining report he was soon to present. The report had been prepared by his juniors, but he had pored over it religiously in the last few days, to ensure he knew every detail, though his computer still held the details of the report in case he was asked some question which he had not already anticipated. *The quotas are on track, and all will be well*, he reassured himself, but there was nothing new to report on the search for the Emperor's mysterious artefact and he would have to evade and promise again and hope that was enough to spare him from the Emperor's formidable ire.

I should feel honoured to be meeting the Emperor in person, he thought. But honoured was not what he was feeling, a vague sense of dread was always lurking at the periphery of his mind in all matters concerning the Emperor and that dread had returned now. Once he had almost fainted under the stifling heat of the pyramid, the pressure of the Emperor's glare, and the thinly veiled threat of the armed black droids arrayed around the Emperor's throne. But that had been over three Earth-years ago, and he had presented this report many times since then. Yet despite his efforts to bury it, still the dread lurked in the corners of his mind.

When he finally reached the imposing black doors, he walked straight past the heavy black droids which ignored his approach and headed towards a small wicket gate set within the door on his right. The wicket gate swung open as he approached, and a white serving droid ushered him inside. *They watch through the eyes of the droids*, he had surmised, but he wasn't exactly sure who *they* were. He ducked his head to enter and straightened up to find himself in the familiar ground floor hall.

Inside the hall, the walls and ceiling were lined with polished, blue-veined white marble with a bank of four large elevators in the approximate centre of the hall which were ferrying groups of ten or more people at a time to the levels higher up within the pyramid. A small tour group was being led by a white droid around the hall admiring the architecture of the pyramid that had taken only five years to build. As they passed Alistair heard a familiar story being retold: "The Sun-God descended from the heavens to Hydrax Prime just over fifty years ago and on recognising the beauty and majesty of the planet, decided he would make it his home and establish himself as the guardian of all mankind in this the fifth era of mankind's evolution."

New residents of Hydrax Prime always came to the pyramid with tourists visiting the main attraction of the city, but Alistair had noted that there had been fewer and fewer residents in recent years as more and more of the planet's industries were being steadily replaced by specialised droids. Humans were far more in abundance and cheaper to replace than droids, but their maintenance costs were much higher. Food, water, wages, accommodation, sewerage, nurseries, schools, hospitals, social venues, police, courts, and prisons all accounted for so much more cost than simply deploying a droid to do the work of a human, more reliably, more continuously, and without ever requiring sustenance, pay, or meaning, and without ever expressing discontent. To Alistair, it was the natural order of progress and mankind would need to find an alternative niche in the new mechanised economy if it was to compete with the fruit of its own creation.

The droid that had brought Alistair inside directed him to a door on the right of the hall and through it to a private elevator which whisked both him and his new escort up to the Throne Room of the pyramid. There he exited the elevator, his ears popping with the change in air pressure and passed through another door and down a narrow corridor to enter the Throne Room from its main entrance.

He swallowed hard and cleared his throat in readiness, *better to be cheerful than morose*, he thought, forcing a smile across his broad freckled face as he walked through an ornate arch into the Throne Room. In the throne room, the floor, walls, and ceiling were all polished gold inlaid with gemstones in complex floral designs. On the far side of the room, opposite the arch through which Alistair had entered, a large dais filled the room from wall to wall and on it sat the Emperor on his enormous throne, the back of which was fashioned in the semblance of a peacock's fan. The fan, like everything else in the room, was wrought in gold, but each eye of the fan was formed of enormous sapphires, rubies, and diamonds. The fan stretched up behind the Emperor's head before fanning out in a wide semicircle to display its ornate workmanship and the incalculable wealth of its splendour. On a red velvet cushion the Emperor sat bare chested, inspecting his audience with shrewd dark eyes. Except for those eyes, his entire body from head to heel was gilded. He appeared to have been painted in gold or covered in gold leaf and his body shone brilliantly even as the daylight from the terraces began to fade to a red dusk. No hint of fat was visible on the Emperor's body and the sinews and fibres of his muscles rippled with even the slightest of his movements. His face was slender and youthful and to Alistair he looked no older than twenty-five Earth-years in age, though he had ruled the Empire for more than twice that time. Standing behind the throne at either side of its front edge, cloaked in shadow, Alistair saw four pairs of red eyes hovering in the blackness and watching the hall.

A broad audience of common folk were on the knees in the main hall before the dais and most were prostrate, bowing their heads to touch the golden floor and mumbling words of prayer from the Emperor's holy Golden Book, beseeching the self-styled Sun God for sustenance, assistance, and deliverance from their difficulties. *They worship him*, Alistair knew, having previously witnessed this display of reverence directed at the Emperor that made him deeply uncomfortable. Some of the folk had brought offerings of fruit and meat to lay in baskets at the Emperor's sandalled feet and all had dressed in what Alistair knew would be their finest clothes for the ritual - shabby shirts, trousers, and dresses of cheap synthetic materials in bright mismatched colours.

"Father, help us!" Alistair heard one worshipper cry out.

"Save my son!", another shouted.

"Father, save us, we beg for your mercy from this disease."

"Please Father, please…hear me! I am your loyal servant! Please don't let them take me!"

He's just a rich guy, Alistair thought, wanting to scream at the fools around him. *Just because a man paints himself in gold, doesn't make him a god. Have some dignity.* At that moment the Emperor turned his head to stare at Alistair with his deep brown eyes that seemed to see through Alistair's skin and inspect his innermost secrets. For half a moment of panic, Alistair wondered if he had spoken his thoughts aloud and that one of the droids had heard him, but he quickly composed himself with a deep breath. He nodded to the Emperor in acknowledgement of their eyes meeting, but still the Emperor stared, unsmiling, unmoving, just staring…at Alistair. He could feel beads of sweat beginning to form on his brow, so he knelt on his right knee and bowed his head in order to break the unsettling stare, casually wiping his brow as he did so. *A humble gesture of fealty*, he hoped.

Craning his neck to look up at the Emperor, he felt more sweat trickle down his back and his shirt stick uncomfortably to him as the Emperor now stood from his seat. At eight feet in height, and rippling with muscle, he looked like an enormous giant towering over the crowded throne room.

"Behold the Great God of the Sun, the Master of the Galaxy, the ruler of the Empire, the Father of mankind. He alone do we turn to for our sustenance and he alone can save us from our despair. Turn to him and be saved." A droid announced in a high clear voice. The droid was fashioned in the likeness of an attractive woman with blonde hair and piercing blue eyes and was dressed in a green silk dress which fell to her knees. *The Imperial Envoy*, Alistair thought. He knew her likeness would also be holding court simultaneously in the hall below.

"Hail, Father! Hail, Father!" the crowd erupted in a chant.

One worshipper who was not chanting stood up from his prostrate position to Alistair's right and shouted at the Sun-God above the chanting of the crowd. "My daughter died because of you. You have taken my work and left me destitute. I have no money for food, for medicine! Where is your humanity? Your mercy?"

The chanting subsided as people turned to see who had sullied their prayers. The man had a long black beard and wore a shabby white shirt untucked over brown trousers and he rushed forward towards the Emperor, pulling a small dagger from his sleeve as he ran, jumping over other worshippers, some still prostrating in rows before him.

Alistair saw the dagger flash as it caught the light of the sun and for a moment glowed like a flame.

The Emperor looked at the man, but Alistair could read only vague boredom on the golden man's face as the black droids began moving, to quickly block the man's path. For a moment Alistair thought he saw a flash of white light in the Emperor's eyes and the black droids immediately took a step back bizarrely allowing the man to approach. The attacker slowed his onward rushing pace and looked at the droids in bewilderment, not sure what to do. He had obviously expected to be cut down by the droids but their sudden backstep had confused him. The Emperor retook his seat and beckoned the attacker forward and when the man was standing before the throne, the Emperor indicated for him to kneel at his feet, but the man did not kneel. Alistair could see he was trembling violently, his shoulders were shaking, and he could hear him sobbing. "You are not my god!" he shouted through his sobs and leapt forwards plunging his knife down at the Emperor's chest. A collective gasp of shock passed over the crowd. The Emperor grabbed the man by the neck with his left hand and placed his right hand under the bearded man's chest. A sudden blast of fire and plasma exploded through the attacker's body, igniting him instantly in flame. The man's clothes erupted in yellow and red flames, whirling and dancing across his back as he staggered backwards screaming in pain and fell to the floor, writhing to escape the flames that spread quickly over his face, arms, and legs. When he flopped backwards to squirm on his back, Alistair could see a large hole in his chest, oozing blood and flame.

Alistair didn't let his eyes stray from the Emperor. The bearded man's knife had clearly made contact with the

Emperor's chest, he had seen that much, but Alistair could not see any hint of a scratch or wound anywhere on the Emperor's bare chest nor any weapon in his hand. The Emperor stood from his throne and stepped over the still burning body of his attacker as the man continued to scream and moan in agony. There was another flash of light in the Emperor's eyes and this time Alistair was certain he saw a small square of light circle the irises of the Emperor's eyes. The black droids began moving again and formed a line across the hall and began advancing from the dais towards the arch of the entrance in unison. The Emperor raised his muscled, golden arms and spoke in a low booming voice. "Clear the hall, this poor misguided man must be tended to." The people were distressed. Some talking and whispering to one another whilst others sobbed or wiped tears from their eyes, as they hurried from the hall. Alistair turned to leave, horrified at the wailing agony of the man still burning behind him, and jostled by the wave of people rushing to get out. A white droid approached him and gently placed its metal hand on his right shoulder. "Not you. Stay," was all it said, and Alistair did as he was bid.

Once the throne room was cleared of worshippers. Alistair made his way to the foot of the Peacock Throne, where the charred body of the attacker was now a blackened heap of burnt flesh, still smouldering, but intermittently twitching.

"Chief Executive," The Emperor's voice boomed around Alistair and seemed to reverberate off the walls of the pyramid in a deep rumble which persisted for a few moments in his ears.

"Your Radiance. I am pleased to see you are unharmed."

"Some of my people offer a sacrifice with the produce of their labour, others choose to do so with their lives. Continue."

"Yes…indeed." Taking a deep breath, Alistair continued, "I am pleased to present the monthly report on the operations of His Majesty's Imperial Mining Corporation." Alistair's own deep voice sounded squeaky and small to him in comparison with the Emperor's booming bass. He sorely wished he had a desk to hide the nakedness he felt, as the Emperor's dark brown eyes bored down into him, completely ignorant of the dying man at his feet.

"Continue."

Alistair cleared his throat and began. He provided a brief summary of the percentage variance from the monthly mining quota of raw materials his company had extracted from each of the colonies, taking each colony in turn and then reporting by each of the three major elements he was charged with collecting – lithium, gold, and uranium as well as some of the lesser elements the company had found. Occasionally, he would glance down at the man beside him, or at his computer, but for the most part he had committed the key figures to memory, and he recited them easily now. As he did so he began to relax a little. *All is going well*, he reassured himself.

"Tell us of Carthage."

"Our mines on Carthage are on track to deliver the quota of each of core minerals as forecast, we have found a rich vein of lithium ore and may even surpass the forecast for next month."

"You informed us you had a contact within the Duke's inner circle."

"Yes. Your Majesty," he answered, as he wondered where this was heading.

"Yet...You do not mention to us that the Duke's own mine has been idle for ten days".

"Yes, that is correct, Your Majesty." Alistair swallowed. His throat suddenly dry. "The Duke has interrupted drilling temporarily it seems. I understand they have drilled into a gas deposit of some kind and are investigating".

"You are not reliably informed...which makes us wonder how reliable your informant is." A furrow appeared in the Emperor's golden brow, and Alistair suddenly felt the urge to open his bowels as a knot tightened in his stomach. "The Duke has managed to do what you have thus far proved incapable of doing."

"The artefact, Your Majesty?"

"Indeed...It appears the Duke has acquired it before you, which makes us ponder the value of your service."

"Your Majesty, we have been drilling tirelessly, we have surveyed the planet from orbit and there was no sign...no geological anomaly...nothing to indicate where the artefact might be hidden. The Duke must have stumbled upon it by chance alone." He could hear his own voice becoming more shrill as he protested and glanced again at the curled up heap of smoking flesh that had been a man at his feet. Alistair had only the vaguest idea of what the artefact actually was, but his previous questions on the subject had yielded little and he was loth to ask again. Certainly not now.

"One does not deal in chance, sir. One deals in strategies and certainties."

"Certainly, Your Majesty. Is there anything you require from me to facilitate the acquisition of the artefact?" he said trying to move the discussion on from his failure.

"Appropriate action has been taken and the artefact will soon be in our possession. Please ensure your staff and all essential mining equipment are removed from the planet within ninety-five hours hence."

"We are to stop mining on Carthage?"

"Indeed. We thank you for your service…And Chief Executive…It is our expectation that our staff will inform *us* of the latest developments in the colonies where they operate, not the other way around. Ensure you have better information the next time we meet."

"Certainly, Your Majesty…Radiance…Your Radiance."

Alistair was swiftly ushered from the throne room by a white droid that might have been the one that had shown him in, but he could not be sure, and didn't particularly care. He wiped sweat from his brow and walked swiftly to the entrance, glad to be away from the Emperor, his stare, and the burning man.

Once outside in front of the pyramid's ebony doors, he doubled over and took several deep breaths to calm himself. He could still smell the bearded man's burning flesh on his clothes, and see his hands clawed and blackened by the fire that had consumed him. He could still hear the man's screams echo in his ears. *The Emperor is invading Carthage*, he thought. *In ninety-five hours*. His first thought was to his friends and staff still on the planet and then another thought came to him.

Alistair left the stone walkway and walked along a paved path to a road that cut past the pyramid. There he waited for a few minutes until he saw the slanted black glass cube of a taxi. He hailed it and it pulled up next to him, its sliding doors parting on the side to allow him entry. The interior of the driverless taxi had a two leather benches opposite one another with a glass tabletop between and a large glass roof that, like all the taxi's windows, were heavily tinted. Once seated at the back of the taxi, he gave instruction for it to take him to the spaceport. He then drew out his sleek glass telephone and dialled his contact on Carthage. The phone rang for several rings but once it was answered the men greeted one another warmly.

"I just met with the Emperor, and it seems the job you did worked wonders." Alistair began.

"Just don't say anymore. This is an open line. Anyone could be listening."

"Okay, okay, take a breath and untwist your panties my friend! You've got nothing to worry about. Everything was done at the instruction of the Emperor's Envoy, and the Emperor is the law. There is no higher authority in the galaxy. You're in the clear."

"Just stop. You don't understand, something has happened here. An Imperial shuttle arrived at the Duke's residence and there has been some sort of commotion. I don't know what's going on, but I need to get back to Hydrax Prime. I don't want the Duke coming for me if he finds out."

The Emperor's 'appropriate action' no doubt. Alistair thought. "Look calm down, I'll get you to Hydrax Prime, or better yet Vega-3, that place is wild, you'll have the time of your life. Just trust me."

"No. No. I need to get to Hydrax Prime. Only the Emperor can protect me if they find out."

"Okay, okay…relax. Take a deep breath. I'll get you to Hydrax, but you need to do one thing for me."

"Oh no! Hell no! I risked my ass getting the last job done. I'm not doing that again."

"Listen this is much easier, much simpler. No risk involved, and there is a lot of money in this for you, if you can get this done. Enough to set you up on Hydrax for life. Listen, you're in the clear. If anything happens the Emperor will protect you, but I need this thing done, it'll be much easier than last time."

"What is it?" Alistair knew he had him now.

"The Duke's found something in his mine north of your city. I need you just to take a look and send me some pics and if it is what I think it is, then I need you to bring it to me on Hydrax. Easy"

"What is it?"

"It's some sort of alien artefact. Maybe a weapon of some kind." In truth no-one had mentioned anything about a weapon, but Alistair had his suspicions. *What else could it be?* "The Emperor has been after it for a long time, that's why we've been drilling up all the colonies, looking for it. Trust me, it wasn't for more gold, the Emperor has enough of that, believe me."

"Aliens? You're serious? There are actual aliens out there?"

"The Emperor thinks so and I don't know why, but he's pretty convinced some artefact or weapon has been buried on the colonies for years. So you gonna do this for me, or what?"

"I want twice what you paid me last time."

"Six hundred thousand? You must be kidding. Forget it I'll get one of the miners to take a look. A rich miner he'll be, I can tell you."

"No. You won't. Not unless you want the whole colony finding out. These guys talk a lot."

"Look, I can give you money, but be real, six hundred is too much."

"Look. Okay, Five-fifty, final offer."

"Three hundred."

"Five -fifty, or you can get a miner."

"Okay…fine. Five hundred and fifty New Dollars!" Alistair said with a loud, bellowing laugh.

"Very funny. I want half now and the other half when I send the pictures. I will bring it if you want, but I need the money when I get you the pictures."

"Fine, fine. Just get it done quickly." *Sometime in the next ninety-five hours preferably.*

"Why? What's the hurry?"

"The Emperor is not a patient man, I just need it done soon, okay?"

"Okay fine."

Alistair hung up his phone and leaned back in the taxi. Five hundred and fifty thousand New Dollars was a lot, but if it was dear to the Emperor, the Emperor would easily pay ten or twenty times that to get it. All he had to do was take it and get away, then let the Emperor know he had it. He would use intermediaries to front the deal and ensure everything was paid in untraceable cryptocurrency. There was risk for sure, but at least it wouldn't be him taking the risk, and then he could retire in luxury on Vega-3, the master of his own little empire.

Chapter 3

Ibrahim knelt beside his mother and the now pale body of his father, careful to avoid the dark red blood that had pooled on the floor. He took her hand as much to receive comfort, as to offer it, but she did not respond, silently looking down at the face of her husband, a face she regretted would forever now be twisted in pain. From an earpiece her son had collected for her, Cyrus was explaining in detail what had just transpired in the residence, but his words were barely reaching her. Finally, as Cyrus recounted Alexion's conversation with the Duke, recorded from the residence's security systems, she was shaken from her thoughts by mention of a meeting on Alsuwayra.

"Cyrus, do you know anything about this meeting, besides the fact it was held on Alsuwayra? Who else was present? Do you know?"

"I'm afraid I do not have that information, ma'am. The Duke arranged a shuttle transit to Alsuwayra Ithnayn 18 days ago and returned the next day. I naturally directed the craft into orbit and back to the surface once it had returned to our orbit, but I have no further information about the purpose of the meeting, or who was present."

Why did he not tell me what was going on? she thought, as Cyrus continued. She knew of her husband's desire to federate the colonies to bring balance to Imperial rule, but according to her husband's assailants, the first steps in this plan had already been taken.

"Duchess, I must make you aware that signals from the Hypernet Nebula indicate that in the last thirty minutes, the Emperor's Fifth Fleet has begun to assemble in orbit around Hydrax Prime." The Hypernet Nebula was a vast system of communication relays that extended between all the colonies and allowed them to communicate with one another over the vast distances between them, and to navigate the void of space.

"So, they are gearing for war...Tell me what you know of the Fifth Fleet."

"Verified information on the Emperor's forces is unavailable, as they have never been used in battle, but what *is* known is that the Emperor's army is divided into six principal legions of which the Fifth Fleet is rumoured to comprise over two hundred and fifty fighter jets capable of carrying mechanised infantry. Hydrax Prime has at least four fully automated factories dedicated to the continuous manufacture of droids, but the number of droids produced on the planet each year, far exceeds the number used locally or traded to other colonies. It is therefore reasonable to surmise that the Emperor has been building an army of military droids, which I estimate could number up to two hundred thousand units in total."

The Duchess looked across at the two huge military droids fallen in her entrance foyer and knew that she and her son had been lucky to survive this assault. A small black bird flew down from some corner of the room to perch on the head of one of the droids, before lifting off again to find a way out of the room. There was no native life on Carthage, so like them, it must have been brought from Earth, perhaps as someone's beloved pet. For a moment she wondered if it had flown in before the attack and how then it had managed to survive the destruction in her living room.

"How many men at arms, have we on Carthage?" she asked of Cyrus.

"Including the police force, we have a total of one hundred and twenty-three men at arms. However, as per our inventory logs, we have only fifty-two heavy plasma rifles, sixty-one plasma handguns, and eleven interplanetary shuttles."

Hopelessly outnumbered, she thought with a sigh. *This will be a slaughter.*

"Cyrus, please summon the Privy Council. I would like them in the Duke's office within the hour. See to it that the droids and my husband's body are removed appropriately but send the droids to Dr Schaffer at the Eastern Military Base, I would like them examined them thoroughly." With that she departed to her bedroom, leaving her son still mourning at her husband's corpse.

The Duchess changed quickly from her exercise clothes into a simple black blouse and suit, once again pausing at the ebony box with the gold clasp. For twenty years it had held her vengeance and she dared not open it again, now. Looking herself over in a mirror quickly, she quickly tied her dishevelled black hair into a simple ponytail to bring some semblance of normality to her appearance but immediately regretted the emphasis it placed on the prominence of her large, slightly hooked nose. *Black will be my only colour now*, she thought remorsefully of her newly widowed status.

Within the hour, the Privy Council had been assembled in the conference room adjoining the Duke's tower office. Three of the four men of the Council seated themselves around the rectangular mahogany table for six, in the centre of which sat a channel to Cyrus, a small round, black microphone and speaker. The fourth council member was Nobuhide who was still being treated for the injury to his arm. The men discussed the afternoon's events in whispers. The Duchess entered the room and all three men stood immediately, their chairs scraping loudly against the tiled floor as they stood.

Chief Justice Ezra Aaronovich was the first to speak: "Duchess, please accept our condolences for the loss of your husband. I am sorry that these events have occurred, but please rest assured that we offer our wholehearted support to you and your family at this difficult time." The elderly judge had a white, closely trimmed beard and a receding hairline of grey-white hair, which was usually topped by a small blue skullcap, but the Duchess noted he had omitted to don it this afternoon.

The Chief Justice had once been a member of the Israeli Defense Force, and when she had learned of this, upon his arrival to her colony, she could feel only disgust for the man. Against her wishes, the Duke had soon appointed him to the highest legal position in the colony.

"There are still some good people in world, Mariam," he had said quoting her words back to her. "He has chosen to live here rather the Jewish colonies. Not all Jews supported the actions of Israel and not all Jews even believed that Israel should have been created in the first place. To judge him on the basis that he did military service once for the country he once made his home, is a little harsh."

"I couldn't care less that he is a Jew, what offends me is that he was a Zionist. He chose to make his home on the land we were pushed out of, which makes him complicit in our suffering. I would like to know where he was when the IDF were bulldozing our homes and bombing our refugee camps. Where was he when their snipers were shooting randomly into the crowded camps and when their settlers were harassing and attacking us on a daily basis? Those bastards killed my brother you know – he was only ten!" the Duchess had replied angrily.

"I know, but didn't that guy get arrested?"

"He didn't get arrested. He claimed my brother and his friends had thrown some stones at him and that was it. No-one would do anything. But he got what he deserved in the end."

"They killed him?"

"No-one killed him. But trust me when I tell you, this Aaronovich is up to something by coming to live here, he will betray us at some point, when it benefits him to do so."

Now, as the Duchess sat opposite the judge and the men retook their seats, he seemed far diminished in both his stature and as a threat to her colony. In the ten or so years he had lived on Carthage, he had studiously ensured that she never had a reason to complain about him and she had to admit, he had always approached her with respect and courtesy. Now as he spoke with compassion, she wondered whether she had judged him too harshly, all those years ago.

"I'm sorry it is necessary to arrange a meeting at such short notice, but these events are unprecedented, and I must urgently request your counsel on how to proceed," the Duchess began.

"What exactly occurred this afternoon, Duchess? If you please," the colony's Chief Treasurer, Hiroto Nakamoto asked. He was a small, overweight, Japanese man in his fifties, with a balding pate, slightly hunched shoulders, and puffy pink cheeks. A thin black beard followed the line of his jaw in a futile effort to obscure his jowls and his circular glasses had a habit of repeatedly slipping down his nose, making the Duchess wish he would just get them adjusted once and for all. Though the room was cool, he gripped a folded Japanese fan in his hands and fidgeted with it as he spoke.

The Duchess proceeded to recount the events of the afternoon and what she had learned from Cyrus but was careful not to mention her husband's clandestine meeting on Alsuwayra. Several times in the recounting she paused to collect herself as the memory of her husband's death, and of her son in peril, caused her voice to quaver.

"Duchess, please don't continue if it is too much. I know I speak for us all when I say the Duke was an example to us all, and we are with you in this hour of turmoil," Dr Zaid Abbas, the colony's Chief Medical Officer offered.

Though in his early forties, Dr Abbas was still a handsome man with a square jaw, striking blue eyes and a muscular physique. The Duchess had known him on Earth, and he had spent many years in medical practice in the US. Since coming to Carthage he had acquired a reputation for indulging in the attention of his female nursing staff, but he was otherwise popular at the colony's principal hospital where he now worked. He sat to the Duchess' right and reached out to clasp her right hand with his left as he spoke.

"I'm touched by your support doctor, thank you," the Duchess responded. *'An example to us all'? Yeah right! I'm sure you think so.* Feeling annoyed at the doctor's presumptuous familiarity, she deftly freed her hand on the premise of drawing a tissue from her pocket and dabbed at her still dry eyes. She desperately wanted to berate him, to smack down the arrogant fool, but she knew his act and his false words were disguised as consolation and she would appear emotional to the other men as a result – so she let the moment pass without comment.

"Now that you know what has transpired, I will add that Cyrus is aware that the Emperor has already begun assembling a military fleet in orbit around Hydrax Prime, which could only mean he intends to bring his armies to Carthage. We don't know exactly what he is planning, but extermination is most likely," she continued.

"With respect, Duchess, we don't know that for certain, it could just be a show of force with no real intention of harm." Nakamoto suggested as he nudged his glasses back into place.

The Duchess looked with incredulity at her Chief Treasurer, anger flaring in her face and voice.

"They came to abduct my husband and kill my family! I do not expect they will do any less for anyone else's. We need to decide what to do. Do we stand and fight the Emperor? Or do we run? And if we run, where do we go?"

Nakamoto sat in an embarrassed silence and began fanning himself briskly. The others looked out of the window of the room or down at the table before them. Finally Aaronovich spoke. "We are far too unprepared for war, to fight. To send any men against the Emperor would be to sentence them all to death. I believe it is better to flee, and I suggest the cave system in the Kirishima Mountains, could provide a sanctuary for the people."

"The Chief Justice is most correct, as ever. I have been to the Kirishima cave system, the caves are deep and difficult to navigate, so could offer some protection, and they are large enough to accommodate the population. The question I have however is, to what end?" Nakamoto asked. "We can stockpile all the food and water we have, but this will eventually run out. We require a more durable solution than simply hiding for some unknown period of time. As soon as we emerge from hiding, the droids will kill us all anyway. So I say we stand and fight with what we have," Nakamoto spoke bravely, having suddenly become convinced of the Emperor's desire for war, but the Council members all knew he had no intention of ever participating in any actual fighting.

"What confuses me, is that if the Emperor wanted to kill us off, why wouldn't he just stop sending water to us? We would be over in a matter of months. Why go to the trouble of sending droids at all to kill us?" the doctor asked.

"I expect it is because he wants a swifter end to us, or he thinks we can get water from elsewhere, or perhaps he wants us alive to be his slaves. There are rumours he has hundreds on Hydrax Prime," Aaronovich replied.

"Perhaps the other colonies can provide a refuge for us," Nakamoto suggested.

"But if the Emperor decides to take the fight to them, then what? Where would we go?" the Duchess countered.

"I agree, so I would suggest a multi-pronged approach. Gather the forces of any sympathetic allies willing to stand with us, whilst at the same time evacuating the weakest and most infirm to Alsuwayra. Alsuwayra Ithnayn is the closest colony to us, so it makes sense to evacuate to there. Anyone else not able to fight and who cannot be evacuated, should then take shelter in the caves, at least until we can resist the Emperor's attacks." Chief Justice Aaronovich's suggestion met with huffs of approval from the treasurer, whilst the doctor countered:, "We cannot hope to beat the Emperor's army. Perhaps if we could understand what the Emperor wants, we could negotiate a solution."

"The purpose of the battle is not to win outright – which I agree, we cannot hope to do. Sure, if we *could* win that is great, but our objective should be to protract the battle. To inflict enough damage to make it unprofitable for the Emperor to continue in his pursuit of war and to provide him with an incentive to negotiate."

The Duchess knew the Chief Justice was correct, but she felt surprised to hear this understanding of guerrilla tactics from him. Pushing that thought aside, however, she continued: "I agree, I think the Justice's plan is sound. Cyrus, do you concur?"

The round speaker on the table began to flash as Cyrus spoke in his typically flat tone. "I concur. Even with allies, the fighting force would still be far inferior to the Emperor's, and I therefore suggest it is preferable to meet the Emperor's forces in orbit rather than on the ground. On the ground, we would be hopelessly outnumbered, but in orbit, the allied forces might at least stand a chance of inflicting significant damage."

"If we are all in agreement then, I suggest we begin immediately. I will reach out to the other colonies to start gauging how much support they are willing to offer. Treasurer Nakamoto, could you and the good doctor begin preparation for evacuation to the caves? We will need to think about water rationing – I don't expect the Emperor will be sending supplies anytime soon."

"We would be happy to," Dr Abbas replied on behalf of the two men. "But one other thing. One of the Duke's miners happened to see me at the hospital this morning and mentioned that there was some major discovery at the Northern Mine. Do you know what that's about?"

"It's just some cave that's been found with some unusual geological formation. Nothing important. Which miner was it?"

"I couldn't possibly divulge that information, even if I could remember his name. Patient confidentiality and all that, you see. Just rocks, hey? He seemed pretty excited. I might head out there and take a look, if that's okay?"

"The cave is sealed off at the moment. It's…err…not safe to visit just yet, but the Duke is…was having it looked at." The Duke had told her about the cave but had insisted it was just a hoax. But there was something about the way he described it that suggested the Duke thought there was more to it, but no matter what she said to pry the information from him, he would not say anymore. She looked out of the window to the bright, merciless sky above and wondered how many more of her husband's secrets she would soon discover.

"What would you like me to do?" the Chief Justice's question jolted her out of her reverie.

"We need to keep everyone calm…perhaps if you could meet with all the community leaders and explain what is happening and that we have a plan? I will formulate a battle plan with Cyrus and Master Nobuhide, once he has returned from hospital, and we will convene again in two days to check progress."

With that, the Council members began departing to their respective places of work. The doctor however, remained seated until all the other members had left the room. He was about to speak when the Duchess began. "Don't ever take my hand again."

"I care about you, Mariam," he replied.

"Why do you persist? You know it will never happen."

"I have always cared about you. You know that's the only reason I moved to this bloody, boiling sandpit. I had a good life on Hydrax Prime, but I gave it up to be with you…and my son."

"Don't call him that, he's not your son."

"Don't keep pretending Mariam, please!" his face flushed, and he spread his fingers wide across the table, pressing them down so firmly into the mahogany surface, that the ends of his fingers blanched white, his mouth fixed in a tight line. Finally, he took a deep breath and lifted his hands, clenching them into fists as he spoke and leaving behind palm prints of condensation on the mahogany. "I want to get to know him…I want us to be together…you need to tell him the truth…I have rights too," he spoke softly, but she could see the anger behind his blue eyes.

"We will *never* be together Zaid, *never*! I can't believe you would do this; Ichiro's body is not even cold and yet here you are trying to move into my bedroom. Get out of my sight before I have you arrested! And if you ever try anything again, I swear I will have you stripped of your seat on this Council and shipped off to Alsuwayra in chains!"

"Fine. Do what you like," he grumbled as he pushed back from the table. His chair screeching across the stone floor as he stood. He skulked out of the conference room without another word, but silently admonished himself for revealing his feelings so plainly and so soon after her husband's death. As the Duchess composed herself, Cyrus continued to listen in silence.

Dr Abbas sped down the stairs of the tower taking a few steps at a time. As he reached the antechamber to a further set of stairs leading into the main reception room of the residence, he caught up with the Chief Justice and the Chief Treasurer who had been making their way down the steps at a much slower pace.

"Ahh, Dr Abbas. We were wondering what had become of you," The Chief Justice remarked.

"The Duchess required some comforting after her ordeal. She and I were once close friends in London, and she often looks to me when she needs some support…or…deep satisfaction. Ichiro was a good man but quite small in stature, if you catch my drift." Zaid waggled his little finger as he spoke.

"I see. Well, I was just saying to Treasurer Nakamoto that I have some concerns about this automatic transfer of power from the Duke to the Duchess. We are not a democracy, but neither are we a monarchy and I think some public consultation is required before the Duchess automatically assumes control over the colony."

"Do you think someone is better suited to the task of leading us, Chief Justice?"

"The Duchess is doing a splendid job, but some formal ratification of her leadership is I think necessary, from a purely legal perspective, you understand."

"Oh, I understand. But I don't think that this is quite the right moment for further disruption. The word about this morning's attack will already have started to spread and I don't think a coup d'état will help just now."

"Dr Abbas. I am not and would never suggest such a thing. You misunderstand me."

"Oh, I understand you perfectly well," the Chief Justice bristled in response and turned. Without a further word he exited through the door to his right and down to the reception room of the residence.

When the Duchess returned to her reception room, the charred remains of her furniture were still strewn across it, but her husband's body and those of the three droids had been removed, along with the shuttle on her doorstep. The small black bird she had seen earlier was now flapping at a window, still looking for a way out, as two maids collected burnt pieces of broken furniture into heavy plastic sacks for disposal. Night had not yet fallen across the colony, but the Duchess was pleased to learn that her son had already departed for the dusk prayer at the Grand Mosque.

The Duchess opened the doors to the main residence and felt the relief of a warm breeze on her face, whilst the bird slowly found its way to freedom, searching for some measure of safety in the foreign city that was not its home. As darkness stretched out across the sky to battle the day, a broad river of stars, began to illuminate the indigo sky. Stars of white, yellow, and blue glittered and shone like a billion jewels of a mighty god, casually thrown across the black silk of the night.

Between them all, the huge red star of the Hydraxian system stared down at her, judging her silently.

Chapter 4

As dusk fell, Ibrahim sat in the central square considering the mosque opposite his home. He had changed out of his traditional kendogu training gear into jeans and a black T-shirt, performed his ablutions, and lingered in the square for a few hours, needing time alone to contemplate the afternoon's attack and his father's death. Now as the *adhan* echoed from the mosque's tall minaret, he steadied his mind, rose from his bench, and walked slowly across the charred cobblestones where the Imperial Shuttle had sat earlier. Whilst he sorely wanted to be alone, he felt it necessary to offer prayers for his father and wanted to talk to the mosque's imam. As he approached, he struggled to keep his memory of the violent mosque attack at bay.

An icy finger of sweat rolled down his back, his breath quickening with each step as the domed blue-grey building loomed larger before him. He passed through the metal detectors with a cursory nod to the two security staff attending there and made his way inside, almost expecting to see the walls scorched and damaged, with broken bodies strewn across the main prayer hall. To his relief however, the hall was mostly empty, with only twenty or so men kneeling or sitting near the front of the hall, waiting for the prayer to begin. A few women were making their way to the women's section of the mosque, but their numbers were also far less than usual. It seemed he was not alone in wanting to avoid the place where so much carnage had taken place so recently.

Ibrahim removed his shoes and placed them on one of the many empty shelves in the open antechamber to the prayer hall and stepped onto the newly re-carpeted floor, patterned in green rows with pale white arches to indicate the places for the faithful to make their prayer. He made his way in and sat aside from the other men, crossed leg on the deep carpet, his back to a row of bookcases on the mosque's far left. Much of the mosque had now been repaired but a scaffold was still up on the side of the prayer hall opposite him, as restoration work continued on the mosque's ornate tiling and calligraphy, but no one was working there now.

Ibrahim looked across at the pillar he had cowered behind during the attack, approximately three feet wide and reaching up to support the blue domed ceiling above, which was ornately decorated with gold geometric and floral designs. Ibrahim had sheltered there when the four intruders had begun firing and the congregation had dispersed, men diving for the ground or whatever cover they could find, to shield themselves from the savage beams, destroying everything they touched.

He looked at where the butcher's boy – Salah, had lain. He had been half covered by his father, a stout man dressed in a shirt and trousers who had tried to shield his young son with his own body. When Ibrahim had seen him, the man's back had been ripped open and his blood blackened by fire, his body burning. Salah had been reaching to Ibrahim with a charred hand, screaming and clawing to get free of his dead father's burning weight. The boy's brown eyes were wide as he pleaded for help, but the orange blasts kept coming. *If only I could have got closer*, Ibrahim thought. *If only I had done something to stop them*, but he had dared not step out from behind the pillar. Fear had consumed him then as orange snake-like ribbons whipped between him and the boy, and a moment later father, son, and the opportunity to help, were obliterated by an orange blast aimed directly at them. *Had I been braver perhaps I could have saved him…It might have meant dying…But at least I would have died saving someone's life…At least there would have been some honour in that.*

Ibrahim could feel his heart racing now as it did then and he struggled to maintain composure, afraid panic would overwhelm him in this public place, as the feeling of fear began to return to him. He kept glancing back at the entrance looking for the intruders who could return at any moment to kill them all again, but only the faithful came. Some members of the congregation began to throng around him oblivious to his distress. They offered as many condolences as they did pose questions. Questions for which Ibrahim had no answers. He did his best to answer politely but the attention and the questions were suffocating, he couldn't think, and he felt his breath becoming ragged as his anger began to rise. He was close to lashing out with his fists and running from the mosque, when the *Iqamah* was called, indicating the prayer was about to begin. The men around Ibrahim slowly dispersed and began forming up in rows behind the imam, stepping forward to fill the gaps to ensure the congregation stood shoulder to shoulder in unbroken rows. Ibrahim took a deep breath and steadied himself. He came to do this for his father, and he resolved to see it through, taking a place in the second row behind the imam, glancing once more behind him to check for intruders, just before the prayer began.

After the communal prayer passed without incident, Ibrahim quickly performed a solitary additional prayer to beg for his father's soul but felt no comfort from the recitation of the Qur'anic Arabic his mother had taught him and which he only half understood. Finally, he quietly approached the imam and requested an audience alone.

Imam Omar was tall black man, in his fifties, but looked much younger. He kept a small wiry goatee but no moustache and had a thoughtful manner in which every word he spoke seemed carefully calibrated before it was uttered. Ibrahim had been introduced to the Imam by his mother, several years ago, in an effort to cultivate knowledge of the religion the Duke had steadfastly refused to accept. To Ibrahim, the imam often seemed to offer the advice he needed, and he turned to him again now to help ease his troubled mind.

"I know I speak for everyone when I offer my sympathies for the loss of your father. How are you and your mother holding up?" the imam began as they settled into his private office on either side of the imam's large grey desk.

"Okay I guess…It's just out of the blue, you know. I don't know why they did this…I don't know if it's connected to the terrorists at the mosque…" Ibrahim trailed off, lost in thought.

"Have faith my friend, Allah is merciful."

"Yeah…sure…and cruel. If He is supposed to care, where is He? Why doesn't He do something to help?"

"That is a good question and I think people have struggled with it for centuries. But the way I see it, Allah deliberately created man with the capacity to do evil, to choose between the guidance He gave us and our darker impulses. The suffering we see around us mostly results from the choices mankind has made. Perhaps therefore, it is for us to solve the problems we, as a species, have created, rather than rely on Him to take away the negative consequences of decisions we make. To put it simply, if there were no consequences, then there would be no choice to make."

"Those kids at the mosque didn't have a choice to make, they didn't do anything wrong and neither did my father, so why should they be punished and killed?"

"You're right, but I wouldn't say death should be seen as a punishment, especially if one is truly faithful or innocent of sin as children are. But only Allah can judge a soul and only Allah knows what the grand design of all this is. Maybe there is some higher purpose, some greater good that comes out of it all."

"Greater good…hmm. You say it's about the choices we make. But Allah already knows what we are going to choose, right? So, if he already knows what we are going to do, what's it all for? What's the point of it all?"

"There is no way anyone can know. Our small minds can't grapple with the superior intellect of our Creator. All we can do is trust that there is a greater purpose for all that we see wrong around us and do the best we can to correct it. Remember, the universe cannot possibly be any other way than the way Allah wants it to be, so we have to trust that there is a greater purpose for all the suffering we see."

Ibrahim was quiet for a moment, turning the ideas of free will and predestination, over in his mind. Imam Omar let the silence settle, often in his experience, silence helped people to express what they were really worried about.

"You know my father wasn't a Muslim…So…would he go to Hell?" Ibrahim asked at last.

"I didn't know your father well, but I had met him on a number of occasions. He always struck me as a kind man who genuinely wanted to do good by his people. But your question reminds me of a saying of the Prophet, I once read. If I remember correctly, the Prophet was asked about two women, one was harsh and cruel to others but was steadfast in prayer, whilst the other woman was kind and generous but was not very pious or prayerful. The Prophet was asked which of them would go to Heaven and he replied to the effect that the woman who was not steadfast in prayer would go to Heaven even though she was not pious. Now, if you think about that, it means the most important test is *not* whether you profess to be a Muslim or whether you bow your head five times a day, it's how you choose to treat other people.

"I think it is also quite telling that the Qur'an bestows its highest title on only one prophet – the Prophet Isa, peace be upon his name…Jesus. In the Qur'an he is referred to as the 'Spirit of Allah'. Now, his greatest lesson for us was love, forgiveness, and mercy towards our fellow man. So, if that then exemplifies the Spirit of Allah, then as long as we live in that way and we otherwise abstain from doing evil, *and* of course remain steadfast in prayer, we should receive Allah's mercies and blessings in the hereafter."

Ibrahim was touched by his words and felt some relief from his grief. Whilst he didn't think his father was ever very Jesus-like, he *was* certainly a good man who looked after others and it was comforting to think of his father happy in the hereafter, reclining in comfort in a lush green garden somewhere. "Thank you, Imam, that means a lot," he said quietly.

"Anytime. Remember, there is purpose in all things. Allah is with you…always. Even in your darkest moments. Remember, *"He is closer to you than the veins in your neck"*. Remember that."

With the Imam's quotation from the Qur'an echoing in his mind, Ibrahim thanked him again and took his leave. He returned to his home across the square, still questioning the veracity of his own faith.

When he returned, his mother was slumped in the armchair his father had occupied earlier, her eyes downcast in deep meditation. She sat upright as he entered, and Ibrahim dropped himself into the armchair opposite his mother without a word.

"How is Imam Omar?" she asked.

"He's fine. Still the same. He offers his condolences."

"And how are you doing?"

"I'm okay…it's just a shock, you know. How are you?"

"I'm sad, I will miss him. But I am concerned with what is coming. The Emperor's armies are assembling. There is going to be war soon and that really scares me."

"What is going on? Why is Emperor suddenly trying to kill us?"

"Don't tell anyone this," she said quietly, looking quickly around the room to make sure they were not being overheard by the two maids, still clearing up. "Your father was concerned about the Emperor's unilateral control over the colonies. The Emperor has been extracting more and more lithium from us, every year, for less and less water each time, and we were struggling to cope. And it wasn't just us. On

Alsuwayra, they were having to produce more and more uranium all the time and on Vega-3, more and more gold. Your father felt it was unsustainable and that the only way forward was to bring the colonies into an alliance to provide some opposition to Imperial rule, so that we could have more of a say in how much water we got and how much each colony had to provide to get it. He didn't tell me, but he attended a meeting on Alsuwayra three weeks ago, to discuss the plan with some of the other colonies. I'm not sure who was there but at least Alsuwayra, and Vega would have been represented. Somehow, the Emperor found out about the meeting and sent his droids. He clearly is not going to tolerate any resistance and now it seems he is sending his armies before any alliance can be formed." *If he had told me about the meeting, I would never have let him go…which is probably why he didn't tell me – the stubborn fool.*

"Okay, so we need to pull this alliance together and get the other colonies to help."

"Exactly. Now more than ever we need their support."

Moving to his side she placed her hand on his shoulder. He looked up at her and she could see the anxiety in his dark brown eyes, which looked so much like her own. *This is hard on him*, she knew.

"Don't be afraid, we will get through this," she said pushing a lock of his too-long hair from his face. "I need you to go Alsuwayra. I will let the Duchess there know you are coming, but I need you to convince her and her advisors that we need their help to stop the Emperor and find out who else was joining this new alliance. There isn't much time. I would go, but I need to be here to prepare for the battle. We're going to evacuate as many as possible to Alsuwayra, assuming they agree, and the rest we will move to the Kirishima caves, but I need to speak with Nobuhide tomorrow. Can you go on my behalf?"

"I can. When do want me to leave?"

"Your father's funeral will be tomorrow, I hate to ask you to miss it, but I think it's best you leave tonight, we don't have much time at all. I know you're grieving son, but trust me…it will get easier, and we will have our revenge…in time." She pulled him closer in an embrace, thinking all the while of her younger brother and how his murder had ripped at the fabric of her family. She knew, as then, that her family needed her strength and resolve now more than ever.

It was almost midnight before Ibrahim departed by shuttle to Alsuwayra. Only Nobunaga, Nobuhide's younger brother, accompanied him. Together they wore military fatigues and carried one plasma handgun each. Ibrahim also bore the katana he had now inherited from his father, whilst Nobunaga carried his projectile sniper rifle.

As Ibrahim set the shuttle on its predefined path to Alsuwayra and began powering up its Alcubierre Engines, an Imperial fighter jet emerged from the planet's polar region. The fighter remained invisible to Cyrus' sensors and unbeknown to the synthetic intelligence, it launched itself in pursuit of the Carthagian vessel as the shuttle leapt to near-luminal velocity, in the trough of a wave of distorted spacetime.

Chapter 5

After the meeting of the Privy Council, Dr Zaid Abbas returned to his office at the main hospital and tried to crush the annoyance he felt with a glass of the vodka he covertly kept in his desk. He poured out a large measure into a glass of finely cut crystal and admonished himself for being so transparent with the Duchess, but he was more annoyed at receiving yet another of her stubborn rejections. He slumped back in his desk's leather chair and, as he sipped his drink, he once again recalled their first meeting in London.

He had been seated on a bench in the open quadrangle of the Guy's Hospital Medical School, puffing on an electronic cigarette and letting loose large clouds of white vapour which rose to mingle with the damp air and the sound of students. It had been raining the evening before, he remembered, and the sky was the cold grey of a typical English autumn, forever threatening more rain. Flat puddles still sat in the recesses of the concrete path which cut diagonally across the lawn in front of him and students splashed through them with fits of spray on their way between lectures or mingling together in breaks.

His back was to the four storey steel and glass building called *New Hunt's House*, but it had not been *new* for many years. In that building, he had just given a lecture to some over-enthusiastic third year students on something to do with the calculation of atherosclerotic cardiovascular disease risk and the impact of smoking cessation on risk reduction. The irony had not been lost on him at the time, but he did enjoy the nicotine and his seniority meant he didn't have to care what his students thought of his habit. A habit he had started whilst in medical school himself. Security guards, however, were another matter. They were invariably ignorant and stubborn and enforced the rules of the campus like donkeys following a carrot on a stick. Most of them he could placate with a flash of his ID badge when he pointed out he was a consultant at the hospital across the small road that separated the medical school from the old hospital, but there were always a few that would get a kick out of laying down the law, an attempt to the redress the poor hand society had dealt them and exact some concession with the small power they wielded. Or occasionally he would run into a self-important colleague, some self-righteous prick physician who would make some comment about setting an example, or risking lung cancer, and he would have to restrain himself from smacking them over the head. Instead, he would turn on his most charming smile and complain about human frailty and his weakness as a person.

He had remembered the pack of cigarettes in kept in the inner pocket of his jacket with a small disposable lighter. It was strictly reserved for those moments when vaping was just not enough and for when he craved the harsh taste of the real thing. He had looked around for the security guards who might intervene if he attempted to light one here. Tobacco after all, had been banned for a year then, and had been banned throughout the campus for a lot longer than that and it was then that he saw her.

She had walked into the quad from the building behind him with a cup of coffee in her left hand and a large blue leather bag slung over her right shoulder. He remembered, she had worn blue jeans slightly faded at the knee with a fitted white blouse, her hair was thick and black, wavy, and long, falling to her shapely bust, and on her feet, she wore shiny pointed black heels adding a few extra inches to her height. She was already tall, a few inches short of six feet with a slim waist, an oval face, full inviting lips, and a slightly hooked nose. He had wondered at her origin, wondering if perhaps she was Indian or Pakistani, but something about her olive skin and wavy hair had convinced him she was an Arab. Calling out to her with '*Marhaba*' he had beckoned her over to his bench. She smiled at his Arabic for 'welcome' and walked slowly across to him. Arabs were a minority within a minority in England, and especially so at the medical school, so their common tongue immediately created a bond between them.

They had spoken for a long time, switching easily between Arabic and English at times, and laughing at each other's jokes. He had soon learned she was studying a postgraduate degree in biochemistry, though he could not discern why anyone would want to study that particularly dry subject. He had offered her one of his treasured cigarettes which she had accepted and together they had inhaled the sharp acrid flavour, whilst watching for the security guards that occasionally patrolled the square. He did not recall their conversation, except for her recounting of her attempt to prove Ichiro wrong about Schrodinger's cat.

"I put my little Muffin in my laundry bin just to prove he was wrong," she recounted.

"Your Muffin?"

"He's my Persian, grey cat. He's very fluffy with beautiful orange eyes. He's the cutest cat, so chilled out and calm, he looks like a little teddy bear, and he doesn't mind if you give him lots of cuddles."

"You will have to show me your kitten, sometime," he said with a smile heavy with innuendo and she had laughed at that, smacking him gently on the arm and cursing him lightly in Arabic.

"He kept insisting the cat would die when I closed the lid, even though there were clearly air gaps in it. But I proved him wrong, he was obviously still alive, and he was scratching and meowing like crazy to get out."

"Yeah…I never understood that theory. It has something to do with quantum physics, but I really don't get it."

"I think these physicists just make it up as they go along, they make up stuff that you can't prove either way and then they pretend as if everyone else is too stupid to understand."

"I'm sure you're right," Zaid had said, sensing that her practical demonstration had irritated her physicist partner more than she let on.

He had soon invited her to dinner at an upmarket Lebanese restaurant, and they agreed to meet again the next day, and the day after that. It was almost a week of meeting and smoking in the quad before he got her to a bar near Oxford Street, and then eventually into his bed.

He had been happiest then as they met repeatedly over the weeks, he recalled, his arm wrapped around her, lazing in bed, wondering if this was love. But after almost a month of regular meetings, she had disappeared from his life, hurriedly marrying her Japanese boyfriend, and soon finding religion. It was in no small part because of her, that he had accepted the job in the Boston, moving away to drown his memories of London, and of her, as best he could.

Now, after the war years, the carnage, and the devastation, some part of him still yearned for her. When he had learned of her son and saw him, he understood the reason for her sudden departure. The boy was clearly his. The boy didn't share his blue eyes, but then the blue gene was never dominant over the brown, but there was no trace of the Japanese in him at all. The boy was clearly Arab and for some reason he couldn't fathom, she had chosen her Japanese boyfriend over him. *I would have married her if I knew about her pregnancy. Maybe*, he thought.

But now that he had had his revenge and he knew, time and caution would eventually bring her back to him, begging. Zaid smiled to himself and took another sip.

Chapter 6

Unable to reach the Duchess Aisha of Alsuwayra all evening, Duchess Mariam instructed Cyrus to continue calling and decided to retire for the night. Dr Andrea Martin had wanted to meet her about some translation, but she did not have the energy for any more visitors. She sat on the edge of her bed with the ebony box from her wardrobe. She paused for a long moment, then unfastened its gold clasp and lifted the lid slowly, knowing what she would find inside. Inside, the box was lined with red velvet, and on it lay a long dark steel knife with a black leather grip. She lifted it from the box, held it across her palms and remembered.

She remembered how she had witnessed the callous shooting of her younger brother and the simmering anger and hatred she had felt. She remembered how she had followed the settler for days to find where he lived and how she had crept across his roof and pried open a skylight to gain entry. She remembered moving silently in the darkness and deciding not to disturb the settler and his wife when she saw the bedroom of their only child. She remembered covering the child's mouth with her hand as she slowly slit his throat. She remembered the look of shock and horror in the boy's blue eyes, as he clutched desperately at his neck, but mostly she remembered the blood. Bright red and warm, it had pulsed from his neck, spraying across the room and across her hands and face, like rain in summer.

Returning the knife to its box now, the Duchess cupped her hands together before her and prayed for the child she had killed. She prayed for her husband's soul and for her son's life, as tears of regret and fear rolled down her cheeks.

That night, she dreamed vividly of their escape from London. Ibrahim had been three and she had wrapped him in blanket and collected a bag full of his clothes and food, and together with Ichiro they had sped down backstreets in an old car he had acquired. They were headed for the channel crossing to get across to the continent and from there to try and find some place safe from the war. All the motorways were clogged with traffic leaving the city, so circuitous back roads had been the only option. For hours they had driven, stopping intermittently in alleyways to refuel from large cans Ichiro had filled days ago in anticipation of fuel shortages. Their electric car had been useless as power interruptions continued across the country as a result of the rioting, and now the rusty little hatchback was their only lifeline.

Mariam had ridden in the back with Ibrahim strapped in his car seat and she ducked down whenever there was a risk of being spotted. Gangs of white men armed with knives were hunting Muslims in the streets, firebombing homes in ethnic neighbourhoods, torching mosques, and looting shops. At first, they targeted shops they suspected were Muslim-owned, but eventually any retail outlet would do for looting and any brown-skinned person would do for blood. Police were nowhere to be seen. The attack on the White House had triggered a nuclear response from an unhinged President, anxious not to be seen as weak to his political opponents, and impossible to restrain. He had struck at the holiest sites of Islam in Mecca and Medina as well as at populations in Istanbul, Tehran, Riyadh, Kabul, and Karachi. Millions of people had died and many more would die soon as a nuclear retaliation was imminent. Fallout was already poisoning the air and seas. It seemed the entire world had been plunged into flame in a matter of days and the environmental catastrophe that followed, was only just beginning.

Most people they passed didn't look twice at Ichiro, but a few threw insults at his foreign appearance, and one threw a half-empty beer glass, and another a brick, which lodged itself in the windscreen on the passenger side, causing the cold air to gust through the gaps in the glass. She had gripped Ichiro's katana then, ready to attack anyone who threatened to harm her young son. But Ichiro had sped away as fast as he could, jumping onto the pavement and knocking bins into the road as he fled the group of bloodstained white men with their dead eyes.

They had eventually left the city and arrived in Kent, continuing on back roads that ran alongside the main motorway heading to the coast. Ichiro was exhausted and in the dead of night they stopped in a village to shelter under a tree beside an empty park. They were trying to sleep in the car when Ibrahim had started crying. No matter what she did, Mariam could not get him to stop. An elderly white woman passing by heard the boy's cries and stopped beside their car. "Is he alright?", she enquired, knocking on the door window, and inspecting the brick half sticking out of the cracked windscreen.

"He's fine, thank you, just tired and cold," Mariam answered, pulling off her heavy coat to place it over the crying child.

"Why don't you come in and have some tea, its cold out." The woman said, her breath misting in the cold night air.

Mariam shook her head to decline, but Ichiro accepted quickly for them both. "That would be most kind. Thank you," he had said. Mariam protested quietly but reluctantly went inside carrying her child, her husband's sword slung across her back, like some warrior princess, ready to defend her son.

The woman had let them into the kitchen of her small semi-detached home, which smelt of stale cooking and disinfectant and there she had offered them baked beans and rehydrated mashed potato which she warmed in an old microwave. An array of pill bottles lined a shelf on the wall, and Mariam could see an oxygen tank on a trolley, in the corner of the room.

"Sorry, I don't have much, the shops being looted an' all," the woman said.

"We are very grateful for your hospitality. You are most kind," Ichiro replied.

"I don't usually let coloured people into my house see, but seeing as you've got the babe, I thought it best. It's a cold night out, and with all this rioting it's not safe, see."

"Thank you", Mariam muttered, ignoring her casual racism, and suspecting that the woman's generosity came with ulterior motives. But she was elderly, probably in her seventies and was not herself a threat to either of them. "Do you live here alone?" Mariam asked, exploring for other possible threats.

"Since my husband passed. It's been six months now, but everyday gets harder."

"I'm sorry for your loss, was he unwell?" Mariam asked as Ichiro raised an eyebrow at her prying, but she ignored him.

"Aye, had the C.O.P.D. I got the diabetes though, does nothing good for my legs." She waved a hand at her thick legs which Mariam now noticed were heavily bandaged under a blue spotted dress that fell to her knees. "Ulcers see. Doctor Rub, he's my doctor. He's one of your lot, see. He's nice though, comes to see me. But every time he's giving me more pills. *'You have to try and remember when to take the right ones otherwise you'll poison yourself'*, he says. I swear if you shook me, I would rattle, I take so many bloody pills. Excuse my French…Now, look at me prattling on, you eat up dear, you're so skinny, you need to put some meat on your bones, or you'll waste away. Eat up while I go get your beds ready."

"We couldn't possibly intrude, you've been so kind," Mariam protested. Though rest was appealing to her, staying in a stranger's house in the middle of a war was foolish. *She might seem harmless, but they had no idea what her real motives were. Better they should sleep in the car in case someone tried to steal it or their fuel,* she had thought.

"Nonsense, its cold out and the babe will catch a chill if you sleep in the car, what with that hole in the glass, like."

The woman would accept no further debate and slowly pulled out fresh sheets which she placed on a hospital bed in her living room and on a velvet settee nearby.

"Don't worry, my Ben didn't die in it," the woman said when Ichiro looked quizzically at the bed. "He died in the chair there", she said pointing to a worn-out velvet armchair next to the settee, which sat opposite the television and had a deep depression in the seat cushion.

"Okay." was all Ichiro could muster as he stared at the armchair.

Ichiro made up the settee and the bed, taking the settee for himself whilst Mariam slept on the bed with the guard rails up on either side, so Ibrahim could sleep beside her without fear of him rolling off.

Mariam lay awake for a long while listening to sounds of Ibrahim snoring softly beside her and wondering what to do if they made it across the Channel in one piece, but eventually drowsiness overcame her, and she slept soundly. The next morning at dawn, the refugees took their leave of the old woman thanking her for her generous hospitality and continuing on their journey south and east. The bombs had fallen the next day and in a few horrifying moments, London was turned into a desolate wasteland. "At least there are some good people left in the world," she had remarked to Ichiro as they took their leave.

She had wondered many times over the years what had become of the old woman, who was surely dead by now even if she had escaped the bombs, but after her experiences in Palestine, she was grateful to have had the encounter with the woman whose name she had never known.

Mariam awoke flustered for a moment, as she checked the time. She pushed herself upright in her bed, rubbing the sleep from her eyes. War was coming for her again and this time she needed to be ready.

Chapter 7

Inside the shuttle travelling from Carthage to Alsuwayra, Nobunaga and Ibrahim were ignorant of the danger that was pursuing them. Nobunaga sat in an awkward silence at the pilot's station, an array of buttons and lights blinked at him from the control dashboard as the pale blue light of the Alcubierre distortion shone through the vessel's front window. He was three years younger than the twenty-two year old Duke's son who sat in the co-pilot's seat. He wanted to be sensitive to Ibrahim's bereavement but could not quite find the words to express his compassion for his friend. As he mulled what to say, he felt the silence hardening between them. "I'm sorry about your dad," Nobunaga eventually blurted, relieved to have finally punctured the silence.

"Thanks…how's your brother doing?" Ibrahim replied. Having already enquired at the hospital after Nobuhide's health, he knew his friend was fine, but he felt the need to stir them both out of silence. Otherwise, it would be a *very* long trip to Alsuwayra.

"He's okay. It's his left arm so he should be back up to fighting in no time. Do you know what this is all about? Why did the Emperor attack us?" he said staring down at the hypnotic blinking of the dashboard.

"Basically, because the Emperor's a bloodthirsty bastard and he wants to kill us all!" he replied, only half in jest. Despite his mother's instruction to do otherwise, Ibrahim decided Nobunaga needed to know and proceeded to brief his companion on his father's opposition to the Emperor and their mission to bring Alsuwayra into the oncoming war. Nobunaga took it all in listening in silence and pondering how a battle against an army of well-armoured Imperial droids could be survived.

"You realise what you're talking about is revolution," he said at last.

"You can call it that. I call it justice. The Emperor killed my father and I want revenge. Are we supposed to put up with him starving us of water? We're not his slaves, we have to fight for our right to live in peace and freedom."

"You're right, but don't you think the Emperor is too strong? How can we fight someone who has thousands of droids?"

"Hundreds of thousands…but you know what? Your brother and I destroyed two of his droids with wooden swords. If we can do that, we can kill a whole lot more with plasma rifles. And if we can get more weapons and more men, we can win this fight".

Nobunaga was not entirely convinced but he said nothing in response, only nodded in apparent agreement. The two men continued in conversation about the war to come. Eventually the constant low hum of the Alcubierre engines, got the better of them both and they retired to the passenger quarters to rest in the comfortable leather recliners of that section.

The Imperial fighter pursuing the shuttle, was enveloped within its own Alcubierre distortion a thousand or so kilometres behind the Carthagian vessel. It was a sleek black vessel with a curved front edge, wide fuselage and a long tail which helped steady the vessel within the spacetime distortion. An array of plasma pulse cannons were positioned within the vertical face of its leading edge, but on board the vessel was empty, it was under the control of the Emperor's synthetic intelligence – Alexion, who would steer it again once its leap to Alsuwayra had been completed.

After travelling for eight hours at velocities just below that of light, both vessels neared the Alsuwayrean system. First Ibrahim's shuttle and then the Imperial fighter dropped out of their Alcubierre distortions and slowed dramatically to a halt. Neither of the passengers experienced any deceleration and the blue hue of the Alcubierre distortions enveloping both ships evaporated instantly. Proximity alarms began blaring almost immediately and the men scrambled to check the shuttle's sensor array finding the Imperial fighter closing in on their position a thousand kilometres way. Sensors indicated its weapons system were at readiness. As Nobunaga powered up the shuttle's short range jets and began preparing evasive manoeuvres, the shuttle's rear outer hull exploded into space and both men were thrown backwards by the jolt. Alarms bleeped and blared as the two men struggled to regain their seats in the weightless environment, fear gripping them both. "Are they firing on us?" Nobunaga yelled, the fear palpable in his voice.

"I don't think so. I think it's a malfunction," Ibrahim replied, the steady red warning lights on the dashboard, indicated a plasma leak from one of the Alcubierre engines aboard. The shuttle was propelled forwards and began to spin. Out of control it drifted closer to the looming blue-green planet, many thousands of kilometres ahead. As they spun, the men caught brief glimpses of the Imperial vessel approaching at speed and closing in on their position.

"No. I think their shooting at us!" Nobunaga shouted.

Ibrahim fired the shuttle's thrusters to stabilise the spin and steady the craft. As he slowly regained control, he turned the vessel towards the planet and engaged the shuttles rear jets, but nothing happened. The explosion at their rear had neutralised their jets.

"Quick, get into your spacesuit, if they are shooting at us, the hull won't hold," Ibrahim instructed. Taking them from beneath their seats, the two men quickly donned blue emergency, single-use plastic and rubber insulated suits, with interlocking seams, and round helmets locked at the neck to seal the inhabitants from their environment. Once fitted they strapped themselves at the pilot's positions and quickly checked their systems and their options. The shuttle was not equipped with weapons, their long-range communications were disabled, and their jets were non-functional. Nobunaga had become silent, unable to think clearly, thoughts raced across his mind in an unfocused whirl of fear and panic. Ibrahim meanwhile took a deep breath in his suit and exhaled, momentarily fogging his helmet before the internal climate system cleared his view. Calming himself, he took manual control of the thrusters and began nudging the shuttle forward as quickly as he could make it go. "Check the sensors, Alsuwayra has two moons, I don't think we can make it down to the surface without our jets."

"I'm on it," Nobunaga replied, the task directing his mind to action. After a moment, Nobunaga spoke again. "Okay, there is a moon eighty-three degrees off to our starboard side and at a declination of fifty-five degrees, it's at a distance of three thousand five hundred kilometres. We may be able to make it."

Ibrahim steered the shuttle towards the moon. Its progress was painfully slow, and they knew the Imperial fighter would be almost on top of them by now. Whether or not it was hostile, the Emperor's attack on the Duke meant they had to be wary of any Imperial vessels now. In the distance he could see construction ships orbiting the planet, their robotic arms manoeuvring large pieces of metal into some type of array.

"I have an idea," Ibrahim said. Open the cargo doors and the seals between the passenger section and the cargo bay. The escaping air will give us a bit of a push. Nobunaga quickly executed the instruction and the shuttle jolted forwards once more, pushing the men backwards in their seats. Alarms blared again to tell them the hull was open to space and oxygen was escaping. Ibrahim fought with the thrusters to regain some semblance of directional control from the sudden acceleration of the craft as it pushed them closer to the Alsuwayrean moon.

Ibrahim and Nobunaga watched their sensor screens as the Imperial drone closed in on their position. Now less than three hundred kilometres away it could destroy them easily. Ibrahim knew there was nothing further to be done, the thrusters were almost spent, and the shuttle was travelling down to the Alsuwayrean moon as fast as he could make it go. Reaching across to his friend he placed a hand on his shoulder and waited for the inevitable.

As the men waited to die, two Alsuwayrean Orbital Patrol ships appeared ahead of the Carthagian shuttle. Moving past it they engaged the Imperial fighter stopping side by side between the drone and the Carthagian shuttle. Ibrahim and Nobunaga listened as the Alsuwayrean patrols radioed the Imperial vessel on all frequencies: "Imperial vessel, this is Alsuwayrean Orbital Patrol. You are now in Alsuwayrean space and are instructed to immediately cease and desist all hostile activities."

"Alsuwayrean Patrol, we have not fired upon the Carthagian vessel and are ready to provide assistance as required. However, we know a terrorist fugitive is onboard and we have been instructed to apprehend the fugitive and return with him to Hydrax Prime. Stand down or you will be considered to be aiding and abetting the fugitive."

"You are now in Alsuwayrean space and the Alsuwayrean government has authority here. You are instructed to remove yourself from Alsuwayrean space immediately. If you do not stand down, we will have no choice but to destroy your vessel."

"Very well, Alsuwayrean Patrol." With that the Imperial fighter shot several volleys of plasma pulses at the two patrol ships. One was destroyed instantly in a momentary explosion of orange and red flame which extinguished almost immediately in the vacuum of space. The other vessel darted and dived to avoid being hit. It flew under the Imperial fighter, turned, and shot upwards at its fuselage destroying it instantly and leaving fragments of the vessel floating helplessly in space.

Ibrahim and Nobunaga both released a deep sigh of relief. Ibrahim continued his shuttle's descent to the Alsuwayrean moon, grateful to be alive, albeit at the cost of the Alsuwayrean Patrol ship and its crew, but unable to comprehend, why the Imperial fighter was pursuing them, if not to kill them. As the shuttle flew over the powdery grey surface of the moon, potted with rocks and craters, he searched for a safe spot to land and finally brought the shuttle down to rest on the surface with a hard flop, which kicked up huge plumes of grey dust. The remaining Alsuwayrean patrol ship landed more elegantly nearby and soon the two Carthagians were making their way across to the patrol ship with their weapons in hand.

As soon as they were on board, Ibrahim and Nobunaga were disarmed at gunpoint and aggressively strapped into metal seats with arms and legs restrained and their wrists cuffed.

"Who are you? Are you with the Mahdi? Why was the Imperial fighter after you? Those were good men we lost, you better tell me!" one of the patrol officers demanded grabbing Nobunaga by the neck and shoving a plasma handgun into his left temple.

"The Mahdi?" Ibrahim enquired. "I am Ibrahim Hazahari son of Duke Hazahari of Carthage, we are on a diplomatic mission to Alsuwayra. Let him go, now!"

"No time to question them now, we'll take them back to base," another more senior officer commanded as the shuttle lifted off from the moon's surface and headed for Alsuwayra.

Chapter 8

As the patrol ship flew towards the dark side of the planet, Ibrahim and Nobunaga could see out of the vessel's side windows, a few vessels gathered together in orbit around the blue-green planet below constructing a vast array of some kind, but they paid it no attention.

On the planet below, they saw wide blue oceans and great continental land masses covered with lush green forests and rocky mountains. Vague memories of the Earth they had once known as children returned to them, as they swept over the beautiful planet so unlike their own.

The vessel soon flew across the planet's principal city – Amegdoul. Entire neighbourhoods of residential housing estates unfolded before them as well as larger commercial buildings and some tall skyscrapers. Ibrahim felt a deep homesickness for the planet of his birth, as well as a touch of envy. The sight of the prosperous city made him wonder whether his father had been mismanaging Carthage to leave it so impoverished by comparison.

As they flew lower over the city, Ibrahim noted a few collapsed buildings randomly dotting its neighbourhoods, fires burning in many of them, with debris and makeshift barricades across some of the streets below. The disarray increased towards the centre of the city and there he could see intermittent flashes of orange light briefly illuminating the streets below and people running in different directions.

The patrol ship eventually approached a large military base on the outskirts of the city, and they swooped past a crop of four tall glass skyscrapers in what was clearly a business district of the city. The patrol ship closed in on the landing strip in the military base but as it did so, an enormous blast of orange and yellow flame erupted from the top floor of the tallest skyscraper, billowing out in rolling clouds to dissipate into the night sky. The shockwave buffeted the Patrol ship, as fire and glass rained on the streets below. "What the hell is going on?" Ibrahim demanded of his captors.

"War," came the only reply.

The two Carthagians were roughly offloaded from the patrol vessel and taken to interrogation rooms where they were separated and made to wait. Both men were seated and cuffed to tables in their respective rooms, and they could hear many shouted instructions and the distant sound of ships lifting off and people rushing. At last, after an hour or so, a man in his thirties dressed in military fatigues, entered. "I am Captain Marwan Abdul-Jabbar. Perhaps you can tell me why three of my men have died saving your ass today?"

"As I told your men, I am Ibrahim Hazahari, son of Duke Ichiro Hazahari the ruler of Carthage. I am on a diplomatic mission to speak with Duchess Aisha."

"Sure, sure...Why was an Imperial vessel chasing you?"

"I don't think they fired on us, I think we had a malfunction, some sort of plasma leak, but I don't know why the fighter was chasing us. All I know is the Emperor attacked our colony earlier today. I need to speak with the Duchess urgently."

"Seems like they were going to fire on in any case if my men hadn't intervened. What do you know of the Mahdi?"

"What Mahdi? I don't know anything about a Mahdi!"

"Why are you carrying weapons? Are you helping them?"

"Help who? I don't know what you're talking about!" Ibrahim shouted in frustration now.

"Okay, okay, calm down. We'll check your story. You just wait here."

"I don't have time to wait around, Carthage is in danger. I need to speak to the Duchess, now!"

"Yeah, that's not going to happen," Marwan said as he left the room to confer with his colleagues. After a further hour or so of waiting, the captain returned. "Okay, it seems your story checks out. We spoke to your AI, and he verified your story and sent us a picture of you and your Chinese friend there. You will get your meeting with the Duchess in the morning."

"He's Japanese and I need to see her tonight, I have an important message I need to deliver in person."

"Sure, whatever. Sit tight, we are in the middle of something just now, but we will be back for you. Just don't leave this room" Marwan said as he freed Ibrahim from his restraints.

"I will have someone bring you something to eat and drink and we will bring your Chinese…sorry…*Japanese* friend in here, okay?"

"Okay, that's fine. But I need to see the Duchess tonight."

"We'll see what we can do."

Nobunaga was brought into Ibrahim's interrogation room accompanied by a tray of two sandwiches in plastic packaging and water bottles for both men. As they devoured the food, Ibrahim paced the room deep in thought.

The sun was rising in the west when a soldier returned to the room with a plasma rifle over his shoulder. He took the Carthagians out to a waiting shuttle and they were soon taken further out from the city towards a wide chain of tall, rocky, grey mountains. The shuttle flew high into the range and then down into a depression protected all sides by the mountain range, landing on an enormous stone pad marked with giant letter S, a few hundred metres from a small concrete building.

The Carthagians were ushered inside the building to a glass-walled conference room overlooking a wider room occupied with around fifty people busily talking into computer consoles and into landline telephones. At last, an elderly woman dressed in blue silk embroidered with gold thread and a scarf over her head, entered the room. She pushed the scarf back off her head, as she sat at the head of table, and black hair streaked with grey, tumbled down to her shoulders. Two armed guards accompanied her, and they stood behind, on either side of her, with rifles at the ready. Her skin was deeply creased around her eyes and mouth, but her blue eyes looked friendly. "Welcome to Alsuwayra. I am sorry my men have held you captive, but we had to be sure you were not with the Mahdi. We are at war with them you see. You're Ibrahim. I haven't seen you since you were a child. You don't remember me?"

"I'm afraid not. I hadn't realised we had met before."

"Well, it was a long time ago, around the time your colony was being established. Your parents came to visit me. You must have been eleven or twelve. How are your parents?"

"Not good. The Emperor killed my father, earlier today…err…yesterday, I mean. He sent some droids, and they killed him. My mother is in charge now, but the Emperor is sending his droid army to wipe us out and we need your help."

"I see…I'm very sorry to hear that. Your father was a good man. He came to see me a few weeks ago in fact. He was concerned about the Emperor. I told him it was unwise to go openly against the Emperor, he is too strong for all of us. And now we have this Mahdi business to deal with."

"There are around half a million people on Carthage, young families with children. They are all facing extermination. If the Emperor send his troops, it will be genocide."

"Yes…I had a faint hope that the brutality of men would diminish once each tribe of people stopped fighting over small pieces of land, but sadly I think it is in the nature of men to find something to fight about. I don't think that will ever change, no matter how far across the galaxy we travel."

"What can we do?"

The Duchess did not reply, she looked down at the table and across at the roomful of technicians, many of whom had noticed her presence and were looking across in curiosity and exchanging whispers with one another. The Duchess paused to consider the predicament, weighing the risks and benefits of an all-out war with the Emperor to defend a minor colony of little strategic interest to her whilst battling an insurgency of a well-armed Islamist group, already at her throat. "I'm afraid, Ibrahim, my forces are already engaged in street-to-street battles with this gang of fanatics, we cannot fight a war on two fronts, especially against as powerful a force as the

Emperor commands. My first responsibility is to this colony and my people look to me for protection."

"There was a terror attack on our Grand Mosque a couple of weeks ago and the terrorists fled here. I assume they are the same, who are these people?"

"They call themselves the 'Soldiers of the Mahdi' and they have attacked us many times. They have attacked our churches and mosques and even blew up a school, killed hundreds of children. So, we launched an attack on them to try and wipe them out. Now they have responded with all-out war, they have taken over a district of the city and are well-armed with many plasma rifles as well as conventional machine guns. We are planning an attack on their base tonight to end this."

"Let me go with your forces. We need to stand together to fight these threats. Let me help you."

"What can you do? I already have an army. I don't need to risk your life too."

"I am trained in combat, I can fight. I've seen the damage these people can do. Nothing would please me more than to avenge the deaths of those they killed on Carthage."

"What about you?" she asked, turning to Nobunaga.

"I'm with him. They've murdered our people and they deserve justice," he said boldly, whilst wondering what Ibrahim was getting them both into.

"Very well," the Duchess replied turning now to her guards. "Take them to see General Faisal. Let's see if two Carthagians can make a difference."

"We will," Ibrahim replied boldly.

As the men were escorted out of the conference room, Nobunaga whispered to Ibrahim, "What are you doing? They don't need our help."

"Creating a debt that hopefully she will repay," Ibrahim replied quietly.

Chapter 9

General Faisal was a tall muscular man with short hair, shaved on the sides, and three deep pink scars running down his left cheek, which gave him the appearance of having wrestled with a lion. He would look intimidating even without the scars, but they seemed to accentuate his fearsomeness. Dressed in military fatigues, with sleeves rolled to the elbow, he saw the men in a private office overlooking the central control room. "So…you puny people are going to turn this war in our favour…huh? I'd like to see that." He said mockingly, his bare forearms rippled with muscle as he lent on his hands in front of the seated Carthagians.

"We will do what we can and are happy to help." Ibrahim replied, trying to sound braver than he felt.

"You want to give your life in service to our colony? If so, I commend it.

"This is going to be a two-pronged attack. There is a district near the centre of our city that has fallen to these fanatics, we will be taking that back tonight whilst you go to Jebel Aswad Mountains in the south. That is where we believe the leader of this group is holed up and you and my men are going to flush him out and take him either alive or preferably, dead. You will be leaving in less than an hour, Captain Marwan will lead and brief you on specifics. Any questions?"

"We had some weapons with us when we were taken prisoner."

"Sure, we will get them back to you and you can have some of ours as well. But one more thing. We are not in the business of baby-sitting, and I don't want you getting in the way or puking up your guts on my team's boots, understand? You will hang back, let my men go in first and only when it's clear, you can go in. You will follow my men's instructions exactly. If you can't do that, the Duchess can find someone else to take you on your little escapade. Agreed?"

"Agreed."

The two Carthagians were taken to rest area whilst one of their escorts went to find their weapons. Eventually, the soldier returned with their guns and Ibrahim's sword and the men were escorted to three military shuttles painted with camouflage colours, waiting on the landing pad outside. Twenty men including the two Carthagians were soon underway. The shuttles flew in close formation around the city rather than over it, heading south towards a chain of snow-capped peaks in the distance, which blazed brightly in the afternoon sunlight.

As they travelled, Captain Marwan explained the mission in more detail, "There is a cave system in the Aswad Mountains that we have been watching for a while. The leader of this group, the one they call the Mahdi, real name, Ali Hassan Al-Sabah, rarely leaves his cave and seems to control his army from there. There is nowhere to land on the mountain but there is a narrow path up the mountain to the cave, so we are going to land near the base of the mountain in a clearing we have made and take the path. Once we get inside, we need to locate Sabah and either take him alive or kill him. Simple."

Marwan passed around several copies of a grainy picture of the leader and a group of several insurgents. The picture had been taken from a distance, but it was clear who the leader was. He was an enormous muscular man who stood a head taller than all the other men in the photo and had a deep scar running down the right side of his face and obliterating his right eye. The other men in the photo seemed to have similar scars and Ibrahim recalled now that the terrorists at the mosque in Carthage had similar scars also.

"What are the Rules of Engagement?" asked one of the soldiers.

"Full force measures. Don't take any chances. Anyone you perceive as a threat is a valid target."

"Understood," came the reply.

"Captain, why do they all have scarred faces?" Ibrahim asked.

"Only Sabah has a true scar. The others draw a line down their faces. I expect it is a sign of solidarity with their leader…or…whatever."

After thirty minutes of flight, the shuttles closed in on their destination, the black snow-capped mountains of the Jebel Aswad range loomed overhead as the shuttles flew low across its foothills, just a few metres above the canopy of a lush forest which grew up to the gradual incline of the mountains. Landing in a clearing a kilometre or so from the foot of the mountains, the men quickly filed out of the shuttle with rifles at the ready, immediately establishing a perimeter around the shuttles. The shuttles were swiftly covered with camouflage nets and the men melted away into the surrounding bushes and trees. Ibrahim and Nobunaga followed closely behind.

Leaving three men behind to guard the shuttles the troops moved quietly through the trees, eventually coming to rest at the edge of the tree line before a rocky incline up into the mountains. After a brief halt, snipers surveyed the route ahead as the soldiers moved forward in formation with Ibrahim and Nobunaga at the rear.

The path up to the Mahdi's cave was narrow and treacherous. Loose stones crunched under foot as the men made their way up two by two, occasionally squeezing past fallen boulders and now and then walking in single file. Halfway up the mountain the path led across a sheer rock face with a vertical drop on the left side. Here the men moved in single file and braced themselves against the biting wind which threatened to hurl them onto the jagged rocks below. The soldiers moved slowly on the narrow path until a sniper leading the troop raised a fist and the contingent stopped immediately and ducked down. In the distance the sniper had seen four of their enemy on the path ahead heading down towards them.

"Take them out from here and we'll drop them down the side once we get to them," Marwan instructed the sniper.

"They could have intel on the Mahdi," the sniper countered.

"Sure, but they could also have comms and in any case these guys are pretty loyal to their leader. Use a silencer."

"Copy that. I'll take them out." The sniper lay down flat on the ground and with its bipod legs extended, he readied his weapon. Through his scope he could see the men moving warily towards them on the narrow path, at a slow pace. After a minute of waiting, the sniper's rifle let loose a series of silenced shots and all four men fell to the ground, one of them falling off the path as he died. The troop soon restarted their careful climb up the path until they came across the bodies. Ibrahim could see each of them was quite young perhaps in their late teens or early twenties and each had a black line drawn over the right side of their faces and across their right eyelids. The bodies were searched and, after nothing of interest was found, their bodies were unceremoniously dumped over the edge of the path. Their limbs flailed loosely as they fell, and their bodies smashed and splattered on the rocks below.

The troop continued their assent as the wind grew colder and more forceful with every hour, and dusk began to fall. Eventually, the path turned to the right into a crevice and the troops were able to have some respite from the incessant howling wind. Ibrahim and Nobunaga were cold. Their toes had become numb hours ago and Ibrahim felt the cold was seeping into his bones as he rubbed his gloved fingers together. Talking little to one another, the soldiers ate hurriedly from ration packs. Marwan soon had the team up to move again and onwards they climbed up through the crevice to a staircase carved into the rock face. There they were stopped by the distant sound of conversation, carried on the wind. Marwan instructed the already quiet men to hush and drop down. With the sniper's scope he could see a low rock wall ahead with a lone sentry sat behind it covered in furs and guarding the dark mouth of a large cave, their destination. The sound of people drifted from the mouth of the cave. There was no way to climb the staircase without being spotted by the sentry and no other means of reaching the cave without climbing up the sheer rock face, a task for which the Alsuwayreans were capable, but not equipped.

Marwan ordered his men back into the crevice to avoid being seen and there he described what lay ahead and outlined his plan, his voice just louder than a whisper and barely audible above the roar of the wind. "We didn't know about the sentry at the top of this staircase that must be new. We're going to strike first with the snipers and then charge up the staircase. Leave anything you don't need here, and we will pick it up on the way down. I want weapons hot and grenades at the ready as soon as we pass the rock wall. Don't enter the cave until I give the order, then fan out and shoot on sight. Don't take any chances. We don't know the layout of the cave so proceed with caution. We will clear each section of the cave system in turn until we find the Mahdi. Got it?"

The men huffed quietly in agreement and made ready. Ibrahim was beginning to get nervous now. Although he had trained for years with the small military force on Carthage, he had never actually been in a battle and had certainly never killed anyone. Now they were about to storm an unknown cave system, on the side of a mountain, in the growing dark, with perhaps hundreds of enemy troops lurking in corners of the cave, ready to kill them. Nobunaga was no less nervous and sat in silence, chewing at his lower lip in thought.

The attack was heralded by a silenced shot from a sniper's rifle, immediately felling the sentry as his part of his head exploded in a cloud of blood, blown away on the wind. As soon as the shot was fired, the troop ran up the staircase two by two and ducked behind the rock wall of the sentry post. Marwan peered into the cave. He could see the entrance to the cave leading away to the right with the dim glow of flames flickering beyond. He could hear the sound of many people talking in the cave but as no-one had yet fired upon them, he knew they still had the advantage. He instructed his men to follow and entered the cave first. A wooden rampart had been built across the uneven floor of the cave and the men walked carefully on it, wary not to allow the sound of their boots from carrying into the cave. Marwan and his men followed the rampart as it turned with the cave to the right and into a narrow passage at the end of which Marwan could see a large cavern lit with flaming torches in sconces on the cavern walls. The cave was filled with a throng of some fifty or so men and women, some standing, some sitting, talking easily to one another, unaware of the threat now closing in on them.

Marwan and his troops crept to the end of the narrow passage then immediately threw their grenades into the cavern and began firing into the throng. The explosions shook the walls of cave and the sound of the blasts boomed all around the troops, echoing long afterwards through the many corridors and deeper caverns of the cave system, the sound slowly diminishing with the screams of dying men and women, their limbs torn apart and scattered by the plasma weapons, machine guns, and grenades. Small stones fell from the ceiling of the cavern before a sudden collapse of a section to the right of the cave's entrance in a loud crash. The rocks narrowly missing one of the Alsuwayrean soldiers, as rock dust bloomed in the cavern for a few minutes. "No grenades from now on. Use only your rifles," Marwan instructed.

As Ibrahim reached the entrance to the cavern, he could see a mass of broken bodies, dismembered limbs and blood splattered all across the cavern walls, across the bodies of the fallen, and gathering in pools on the cavern floor. Sounds of moaning emanated from the piles of bodies but none of the Alsuwayreans made a move to recover anyone still living. The bodies he could see were charred black by the fire of the plasma weapons, and some were still smouldering, their faces disfigured and distorted by the explosive blasts, or forever frozen in silent screams of pain.

Ibrahim thought he saw the butcher's boy again amongst the pile of bodies and he felt anger rising within him again. He approached the child and lifted his blackened body from beneath a woman clearly trying to shield him from the carnage. As Ibrahim lifted the child, he could see tear stains on the boy's dusty cheeks and a deep gouging wound on the boy's abdomen. Unable to contain himself further, Ibrahim shouted at Marwan. "What the hell is this?! You're killing innocent people!"

"Shut the hell up! We have our orders. There are no innocents here," Marwan shouted back.

"What did this kid do?"

"You're here as a courtesy. If you can't shut the fuck up, you can go back to the shuttles,"

"Fuck you, Marwan, you bastard!" Ibrahim shouted back, drawing his handgun to point at the captain.

Marwan brought his rifle to bear on Ibrahim then instructed his lieutenant, "Jamal, disarm this fool and his friend. Keep them here until we return. We still have a job to do. Dumb fuck!" he spat the final words at Ibrahim and turned to gather his men.

Ibrahim placed the boy gently on the ground as both he and Nobunaga were zip-tied in plastic handcuffs with their arms behind their back. Their weapons were taken from them and laid to the side, a few feet away, as they were roughly seated in a dark corner of the cavern. Jamal snarled at them with derision as he sat alongside them, whilst the others all moved further into the cavern and into a dark corridor at the rear of the cave.

The captives sat in silence, as Ibrahim looked across the bodies in front of him, the smell of burnt flesh reminding him of the carnage at the mosque. *I'm sorry Salah*, he thought. But as his anger ebbed, he cursed himself for his outburst and for drawing his weapon. He needed the Alsuwayreans, and this blunder could cost him, his mother, and his colony, dearly.

Chapter 10

Ibrahim watched as the Alsuwayrean soldiers were enveloped by the darkness of the deeper cavern system beyond as they made their way forward to find their target. Jamal sat in silence near them resting his rifle across his crossed legs.

"The Mahdi must have heard the attack he couldn't still be here," Nobunaga said after a few minutes.

"They'll find him. There is only one exit from this cave system as far as we know, and we just came through it," Jamal offered in reply.

The sound of distant rifle fire echoed through the cave to meet them, followed by the high whine of plasma rifles and the faint sound of screams. "See. They've already found him," Jamal said triumphantly.

The men waited for the soldiers to return and carry out the body of the Mahdi to prove his death, but no-one came. Minutes slowly passed with all three men fixed in attention on the dark corridor into which the Alsuwayreans had departed. Jamal repeatedly checked his wristwatch, counting time. After a further half an hour, with no further sounds from the cave, Ibrahim finally broke the silence, "Don't you think we should go after them and check they are okay?"

"What do you care, dumb fuck? Anyway, our orders were to stay here until they return, if we go off and make a wrong turn, we could end up lost in the caves. And then it's my ass on the line for screwing up."

"They could be injured or captured. We can't just sit here," Ibrahim insisted.

Jamal sat in silence contemplating. He was only a few months out of the Alsuwayrean military academy and was supposed to be on leave with his young wife, not stuck in a dark, damp cave surrounded by the dead, babysitting two foreign soldiers. He had been called back from leave to assist in the war effort when the Mahdi's forces had counterattacked and despite his inexperience, Captain Marwan had felt he had done a good job so far in his first real taste of battle. He had no desire to screw that up.

Ibrahim continued, "Look if they're injured or captured, and you're just sitting here letting them die, then it's on you. General Faisal will kick your ass, you know it."

Jamal considered him for a moment then replied. "Okay, let's go. But you to better not try anything. I'm in charge here. You follow my orders. Got it, dumb ass?"

"Sure. We're all on the same side here, okay," Ibrahim replied, ignoring the taunts, and pleased to be doing something at last.

Jamal freed the Carthagians from their restraints and they quickly gathered their weapons and made for the dark caves beyond. There was no wooden rampart in the deeper cave system, and they moved carefully across the rocky cave floor. Jamal held the only electric torch between them, and he used it sparingly to prevent the light from being seen by some hidden enemy.

The corridor had clearly been cut from the rock wall of the cave into a smooth oval and descended downwards from the main cavern in a relatively straight unbroken line. Sconces were positioned at intervals along the walls but the wooden torches they held were all extinguished. Intermittently along the corridor's length, heavy woollen coverings hung from the ceiling covering side rooms. The three men checked each of these in turn as they passed them, looking in quickly for their colleagues or any of the Mahdi's people. The side rooms were sparsely decorated but comfortable rooms for the Mahdi's people with beds side tables and some trays with metal teapots.

Finally, the corridor branched into two further tunnels and the men listened silently for any sound of their colleagues. Jamal could not decide which to take, until Ibrahim at last took a decision for them all. "I'll take the one on the right, Nobu, you stay with Jamal." Ibrahim trusted Nobunaga's judgment over Jamal's and felt the two were better off together if the three of them were to split up.

Ibrahim made his way carefully down the dark tunnel on the right. But without Jamal's torch, the way ahead was impenetrably dark, so he turned back. In the disappearing light of the torch, he quickly collected an extinguished torch from a wall sconce in the main corridor and drew his plasma handgun. Pointing the weapon away to the side of the torch he fired it momentarily and torch lit up immediately in yellow and red flames which writhed in the dark and illuminated the rocks to cast dark shadows all around him. Now armed with a source of light, he made his way down his chosen tunnel.

It appeared to be a natural tunnel almost four feet wide with uneven sharp rocks jutting from the walls, an uneven floor and occasional stalactites hanging from the tunnel ceiling. Water dripped slowly from the ceiling around him. The walls of the tunnel narrowed in places and there Ibrahim slung his katana across his back and squeezed past the boulders. As he was squeezing past a large boulder he paused and fell silent. A distant moan had broken the incessant sound of dripping water and he froze, holding his breath and straining his ears for any hint of people ahead. The flickering of shadows gave movement to the rocks and more than once Ibrahim thought he spied a figure moving between the rocks up ahead. He extinguished the torch he held in a puddle of water at his feet and began groping his way forward in the utter darkness, careful not to allow the katana on his back to clang against the rocks as he passed.

Eventually, after what seemed like an hour of groping a path in the dark, he heard the sound of people talking and saw a dim light ahead. A few metres further on and he felt the air become less damp as the tunnel opened into dimly lit cavern illuminated by two electric lanterns perched on a rocky ledge on its far side. Ibrahim could see the silhouettes of soldiers on their knees in the far side of the cavern surrounded by a group of five men standing around them and clearly carrying rifles.

He considered going back to find Jamal and Nobunaga. Although he had no idea where to find them, getting their help would be preferable to fighting five armed terrorists alone with only a handgun and a sword. He was about to make his way back into the dark tunnel he had entered from, when a tall man entered the cavern from behind a wall hanging on the cave's far side. Although he could not make the man's features, he could tell from his height and build that this was the man they had been looking for – the Mahdi. The man moved towards the men still kneeling on the floor and slapped one across the face with a hard slap which echoed through the cave. "So, Capitan, where is the Duchess hiding? Are you going to tell me, or shall I start cutting off fingers and toes?" he said, his voice mocking.

"I don't have that information. The Duchess is moved around from place to place to keep her safe and we are not privy to the planned movements," one of the captives replied and Ibrahim recognised it to be Marwan.

"So, *you* will tell me the places she moves between and the frequency of her movements."

"I don't know it, none of us do."

"Then I guess its fingers and toes then," the Mahdi responded. "Shall we start from left to right or right to left? Do you have any preference? No? Okay, let's start with you and then move left to right." he let out a brief chuckle as he drew a large machete.

"Please, we don't have the information you want. We're all brothers here!" Marwan shouted. His voice pleading for mercy from the pain to come.

"You come into my home and slaughter my people without so much as a warning and you expect me to take it and embrace you as a brother! You are murderous infidels who deny the truth, yours is the hellfire to which I will send you. Take him." The Mahdi indicated to one of his men and Marwan's left arm was stretched out in front of him. "You know I am not a very patient man. I was going to take one little finger at a time but now I feel I can't be bothered with that, so I am going to take your whole hand, then the other one, then your feet. If you tell me what I need to know I will stop, if not, once I have taken your feet, I will start on your friends and once they are all handless and footless, I will leave you here to die of starvation in this damp cave. What do you think? Do you feel like talking now?" he peered down at Marwan bringing his face so close that their noses almost touched.

Still Marwan only begged for mercy and then began reciting from the Qur'an. As the Mahdi swung his sword down onto the captain's wrist, Marwan let loose a curdling scream of pain. "So, do you feel like telling me what I want to know now?" he asked mockingly.

"I don't know anything. I don't! Please!" Marwan replied, his voice breaking with pain.

The Mahdi lifted his weapon to swing again, but this time, Ibrahim fired his handgun, lighting up the cavern in bright orange light as he shot at the man, but missed. The Mahdi's five soldiers returned fire with bullets spraying the cave in Ibrahim's direction. They were blind beyond the glow of their electric lights but now had his general direction for aim. The sound of gunfire was deafeningly loud and echoed and boomed across the cave. Ibrahim dived for cover behind large boulders and scrapped his right knee against the sharp edge of a rock as he lay still. Torchlight began searching over the rocks for him as the constant gunfire died down and was replaced by occasional short bursts. Rocks near him exploded in splinters as the bullets landed.

Inching his way slowly he felt his way around the cave's periphery making his way closer to the captives under cover of the darkness beyond the torches that hunted for him. Three of the Mahdi's men slowly began making their way towards Ibrahim's original position, one held a lantern and lit the way for them, whilst the others shone their torches from left to right across the rocks looking for any sign of the intruder. Ibrahim had already halved the distance between him and the captives now and he was drawing closer with every passing minute.

The Mahdi decided to interrupt his interrogation and disappeared behind his wall hanging into the rear of the cave, leaving only two men guarding the Alsuwayreans. Ibrahim seized his chance. He sprung forward from behind a large boulder and ran headlong at the captives and their two guards, his feet splashing as he leapt through puddles of water and over sharp rocks. As he emerged into the light of the electric lantern, he struck at one of the soldiers with his sword cutting the man across the neck. He fell to the ground without a scream, a widening pool of blood spreading from his neck. The other guard raised his rifle to fire but before he could do so Marwan kicked the man in the leg and Ibrahim fell upon him, slashing him across his arm and stabbing the man through the chest.

Across the other side of the cave, the three men searching Ibrahim's original position now began making their way back to their captives, aware that something was wrong. Ducking behind the kneeling men, Ibrahim quickly freed the Alsuwayreans from their restraints and left them to deal with the remaining three guards. He paused for a moment at the bodies of dead terrorists. These were the first people he had ever killed, but to his surprise he felt nothing. No guilt, no anger, no pride at their deaths, just a looming indifference. He turned to the wall hanging behind which the Mahdi had escaped and began his pursuit.

Ibrahim pulled back the curtain to reveal a comfortably furnished room which a bed to one side and an array of computers and servers on the other with a low hexagonal trestle supporting a brass tray, in the centre of the room, upon which a silver kettle and two glass cups had been placed. At the room's rear a narrow gap in the cave wall led to a deeper section of the cave and Ibrahim squeezed himself through, leading with his left side, his gun in in his right hand, at the ready. *If I could have just got closer*, his thoughts returned to the butcher's boy at the mosque and his own fear of death then. *Not this time*, he vowed. *I won't let him kill any more.*

Into the deeper cave he pushed and ahead he could see a faint light reflected off the rock walls, their surface slick and shimmering under the flickering light. The torches in this section of the cave were extinguished also and Ibrahim lit one again with his handgun to provide some light in the darkness which surrounded him. With the flaming torch in one hand, gun in his other, he slung his katana across his back and made his way quickly across the rocky boulders that comprised the cavern floor. He could see he was nearing on the light ahead which did not appear to be moving away. At last he could see the light was from a lonely torch still held in its sconce on the wall. As he moved towards its light a rifle crack echoed around him and he saw a fragment of rock shatter beside him, sending shards of rock flying in all directions. He ducked immediately and another bullet narrowly missed him, but this one ricocheted off the rock wall and caught him in his left thigh.

The pain was searing, it felt as if he had been stabbed with a hot poker, a momentary sharp stab of pain was followed by a tidal wave of burning as it washed over him an instant later and his leg was on fire. He quickly dived behind some low rocks, chaffing his right knee again on the sharp rocks as he lay on the ground trying to contain the pain and not to cry out. Footsteps approached him now and he knew the Mahdi was watching for movement. Eventually the footsteps receded, and Ibrahim looked out from behind his low rock wall in time to see the Mahdi disappear into a tunnel with a torch in hand. Slowly, steadily, he rose to his feet. He carefully cut the sleeve of his fatigues at the shoulder, with his sword and ripped the sleeve into a makeshift bandage, wrapping it around his injured thigh and tightening it hard to stem the blood oozing from his wound. Leaning on his sheathed katana, he paused, weighing whether to go on or turn back. He was sorely tempted to turn back and seek help from the Alsuwayreans for his injuries, but he felt he owed it to Salah, the butcher's boy, to pursue the man. So he pressed on, using his long katana as a crutch to limp carefully between the boulders and rocks of the cave floor. As he turned the corner the Mahdi had taken, the cave opened once more into a large open space, a fresh breeze blew on him. For a moment he thought he was too late, and that the Mahdi had escaped through some other exit from the cave system. But a light suddenly illuminated the cave and cast a yellow globe of flickering light a few feet from its source. Across from him near the centre of the cave, where the floor was flatter, he could see the Mahdi had lit a flaming torch with a lighter and was seated on a low rock apparently waiting.

"Welcome young man. I see I managed to catch you with my gun after all. I was afraid I had missed," the Mahdi said in a polite tone, eyeing Ibrahim's leg wound with his one good eye. The Mahdi's right eye was obliterated by the deep scar that ran from this forehead to his jaw, the empty socket was red and scabbed and left eye looked unnaturally large.

"No, you got me," Ibrahim replied, the pain in his leg was searing with each movement but he kept it from his voice as best he could, trying to sound unharmed.

"Who are you? I don't think you are Alsuwayrean are you?"

"No, I am from Carthage, my name is Ibrahim."

"Well Ibrahim of Carthage, *Assalamualaikum*." The Mahdi offered the traditional Arabic greeting wishing peace upon his guest.

"*Walaikumassalam,*" Ibrahim replied appropriately, wishing peace upon the Mahdi in return. "Why are you fighting the Alsuwayreans? They say you blew up a school and have killed hundreds of children. Your people also attacked our mosque on Carthage, you killed thirty-eight people there all Muslims."

"The school was unfortunate. They have killed hundreds of my people and our children are of no less worth than theirs, so we took the school to teach them this fact. I had no desire to kill them, but when the Duchess chose to attack rather than talk, I had no choice. They were innocent, I will grant you, but to the innocent child is granted the splendour of heaven without trial, and so really their death is better for them. As for the so-called Muslims I have killed, those who oppose the word of Allah cannot regard themselves as Muslims. These people don't follow the laws of Islam, they follow the commands of the infidels who raped our lands and our women, they are not Muslims. The infidels invaded our lands, stole our wealth, and murdered our people. And where were our great leaders when this was happening? They were getting drunk, gambling, and whoring with their infidel friends, spending the wealth that Allah has gifted them, on lavish trinkets, boats, and jewels, while their brothers and sisters were starving and dying at the hands of their infidel friends. They all deserve death so they can burn in the Hellfire forever, and I will give it to them. And here, what happens here? We were supposed to be the regents, the rulers of the planet Allah created for us, but the infidels and our impotent leaders destroyed it, and now we have to live out here under the rule of this Emperor who wants only to be worshipped as some false god. He deserves death more than any other, for his heresy…though he does have his uses.

"I am the one who will bring peace to all the places where Muslims now live in poverty and war, and I will establish my caliphate on this colony, a true nation in which Islam rules supreme. That is why we attacked the mosque on Carthage. Your people are led by an infidel who does not even believe in Islam, and what they preach in your mosque is a deviation of the faith, an innovation of the religion, that is why it had to be destroyed."

"You didn't destroy it. It is still strong as ever."

"We will in time and then the people will rise up and reclaim what is rightfully theirs."

"So, you're the Mahdi, the messiah who will save us all and bring us back to the straight path to god?"

"I am, yes...and I will prove it. You cannot kill me; you cannot even harm me. I am protected by Allah himself!"

"I can kill you," Ibrahim said casually. He was annoyed by the man's callous arrogance. He wanted to end him here and now. No true man of god would kill innocent people and this man was clearly no messiah. Fear had left him, he realised, and he felt strangely at peace despite the throbbing pain in his leg. He couldn't help Salah now, but perhaps by stopping this man he might save someone else and atone for his inability to help the boy then.

The self-proclaimed Mahdi, beckoned to Ibrahim. "Okay then, but any fool can pull a trigger, let's see if you know how to use that sword of yours and…when you die, this will prove to you that I am the Mahdi. Throw your gun aside." Ibrahim set the weapon down on the rocks beside him and drew his katana in readiness, trying to balance as best he could on his injured leg.

The Mahdi drew his large machete. The dark steel of the weapon glinted in the torchlight and shone as if the Mahdi gripped fire. "I'm sorry to kill you, boy, you have spirit, I can see," he said as he came in closer then suddenly leaping forward in an attack. Ibrahim wobbled on his feet slightly but parried the overhead blow easily. The blows came quick and hard then, one after the other, as steel clashed on steel. Ibrahim's right arm shuddered as he absorbed the impact of each. An overhead downward cut was followed by a slash on his right side, forcing Ibrahim to move left, pain shooting up his leg as he placed his weight on it. He almost cried out in pain as his leg threatened to give way, but he quickly regained his balance to block another downward cut. Slowly they whirled in the dancing light of the torch, breaking apart and coming together as their blades kissed, sparks flying again and again from the impacts and both men grunting with the effort of the blows.

Ibrahim hesitated to commit to attack, unsure of his leg's support. He could feel blood trickling down his leg and every movement was a fresh poker in his thigh. It felt like several minutes of constant resistance to the Mahdi's attacks until the Mahdi at last settled into a rhythm and let down his guard.

The man swung down a hammering overhead blow but as Ibrahim deflected it, the Mahdi was a moment too late in recovering his stance and Ibrahim pounced. He leapt forward striking at the Mahdi's chest with his katana putting all his weight behind the sword and plunging the hardened Japanese steel, deep into the man's chest. Blood oozed from the wound as a foot's length of the bloodied end of the sword poked out of the Mahdi's back. Ibrahim let go of the handle and wobbled to the side before seating himself on a high rock, knowing the battle was over. The Mahdi staggered backwards and fell to his side against the rock floor, clutching at the handle of the sword, gasping for breath, his face a portrait more of shock than pain. Ibrahim stood again and limped forward. Grabbing the sword by the handle, he twisted it and heard the crunch of ribs cracking before he pulled the sword from the wound. Dark blood, black as oil in the dim light, sprayed from the man's chest across Ibrahim and across the cavern's rock walls. As the Mahdi collapsed to the ground, blood pulsing from his chest in thick waves, Ibrahim slumped down beside him to rest. "I told you I would kill you," he said with a satisfied smile.

After a minute or so, the Mahdi's breathing became more laboured and he gasped for breath, struggling to say something he reached out to Ibrahim and grabbed hold of his arm. Ibrahim leaned over him to hear what he had to say, but as he did so, the Mahdi slashed at Ibrahim's neck with his right hand. On his index finger he wore a large metal talon, which Ibrahim had not noticed before in the low light of the cave. Now it caught him squarely across the neck and he was cut from the middle of his neck almost to his right shoulder. The Mahdi's hand dropped limply to his side. He stared at

Ibrahim as he died, a knowing smirk at the corner of his mouth.

Ibrahim pushed backwards from the dead man and grabbed the wound at his neck to stifle the blood that was now gushing between his fingers. With one hand, he freed the makeshift bandage at his thigh and pressed it at his neck but was already feeling lightheaded as the room began to swim and spin around him. He leaned backwards against a rock but missed and toppled to his right side before rolling onto his back and lying flat on the rock floor. Exhausted by the climb up the mountainside, the bullet in his leg and the battle he had fought, he could scarcely move or call out, as he felt strength leaving his body. The cave began to grow darker, and he thought he could see stars in the cavern roof but at the back of his mind he knew he was dying now.

He pictured his mother, her beautiful raven hair cascading down her face and his father laughing uncontrollably at some joke Ibrahim had told. Then he remembered something he had almost forgotten, *"Remember,"* the Imam had said, *"Remember, that Allah is closer to you than the veins in your neck."* In a whisper, he called to Him now.

"If you truly are closer to me than my veins, be with me now, my Lord". He closed his eyes and an ocean opened beneath him and he drifted into it slowly, warm water enveloping him and carrying him gently away as he lost consciousness.

Chapter 11

The Eastern Military Base deserves a better name than the one it has, Duchess Mariam thought as she made her way to the four storey office building that served as headquarters of her small military contingent. She mused about renaming the base after her husband, but military installations were typically named after great warriors in military history and her husband was certainly no warrior. Besides, Carthage had precious little of history at all, let alone any of it militaristic. That would soon change, though, she knew. The Emperor would be invading soon. *Perhaps the coming battle would lend some feat of valour to the base's name...If, of course, there is anyone left alive to rename the base.*

Outside, five large hangars, capable of housing at least two interplanetary shuttles each, were busy with people coming and going, pushing small trolleys of tools with them, or manoeuvring forklifts of bulkier equipment into the buildings to repair and modify the small fleet. The air has hot and dry, and the wind threw hot red dust across her face as she pushed open the glass door of the building. She was greeted by a blast of air from inside as she entered and felt the cool wash over her. The Duchess asked a woman dressed in military fatigues for Dr Schaffer and was soon directed up a flight of stairs and along a narrow corridor to an empty meeting room on the first floor, furnished with a large faux mahogany table and four swivel chairs. The windows opposite the door looked out over the landing strip and the tall, black mountain range beyond. She moved to the window and tried to imagine what it would be like in the caves. She had visited them only once before with her husband who, waxed lyrical about the basic geology he could discern from the red, brown, and black formations within. His enthusiasm however was wasted on the Duchess who could only appreciate the enormous size of the caves. The caves had been deep and dark with many tunnels hinting at further, deeper crevices and caves beyond. Fitting her populace into the caves would be relatively easy, she thought. *Keeping them alive once they were there, will be more difficult.* Stockpiling of food and water in the caves was already underway however, according to the latest update she had received from Treasurer Nakamoto. Dr Abbas had identified the members of the populous most appropriate for evacuation to Alsuwayra based on their age and infirmity, but she had not yet heard from Ibrahim and was growing increasingly concerned at the silence. Her attempts to contact the Duchess Aisha had proved equally unsuccessful. Alsuwayra was integral to their survival. *If Ibrahim has failed to sway the Duchess, he will have to evacuate the infirm to the caves instead. Where is he?* she thought.

She turned at the sound of the door behind her opening and the walking commotion that was Dr Elizabeth Schaffer entered the room. She was a short, portly woman with long tangles of unkempt grey hair which fell to her shoulders and large thick glasses that seemed to magnify her dark brown eyes. She wore a simple white blouse decorated with blue and brown polka dots under a light grey jacket with deep creases at the elbow and dark blue trousers that clung to her broad hips and thighs. Under both arms she carried thick wads of paper and a tablet computer that she dumped heavily onto the table before her. An aroma of tobacco followed Dr Schaffer into the room and as the two women shook hands, the Duchess noticed the distinct yellow staining of nicotine on the scientist's right index and middle fingers and on her large, uneven, and slightly protruding, teeth.

"Duchess. My dear. Have you been waiting long? I'm sorry to have kept you waiting, there is so much to do…so much to do," she said as she popped a mint into her mouth.

"No need to apologise, I was early in any case. But yes…there is much to do," the Duchess replied, grateful that the scientist had the self-awareness to use mints to obscure the smell of tobacco on her breath. A smell that momentarily reminded her of Zaid.

"May I offer you tea, coffee, water?" Dr Schaffer indicated a seat for the Duchess and the women sat across a corner of the table.

"No, thank you, but please go ahead."

"If you don't mind, I haven't yet had my morning cup and I am atrocious without it." She pushed a button on a telephone on the table before her and requested a coffee with milk but no sugar from a man on the other end. "Must cut the calories where we can." She said with a smile, returning her attention to the Duchess as she powered up her small computer.

"I have examined the droids as you requested and there is much to report. The two military droids, let's start with them."

"Please, go ahead."

"Well, their armour plating is three oh one steel, the type that used to be used in tanks of old. Its tough stuff difficult to cut through even with a plasma gun and not easily damaged by small arms projectile fire either." As she spoke, Dr Schaffer projected holographic images of her subjects from her small tablet computer, flicking through a series of prepared images to demonstrate what she was referring to, whilst simultaneously rifling through the papers piled before her. "The head units are where the processors are housed, as one would expect, and Master Nobuhide did a splendid job of destroying the circuits in one of the droids with his wooden sword. In truth, though, he was lucky. The metal seam at the neck of that droid had been damaged and allowed him to slip his stick in here, you see. But the other had been sealed tight."

"I managed to cut the head off the other one, with a plasma handgun."

"Yes, the neck of the droid is vulnerable, and your blast burned through the weaker lobstered steel at the neck, but had you been aiming at its chest it would have taken you at least two minutes of continuous fire to make a dent there and I'm sure the beast would have fired back in that time."

"I see," the Duchess knew she was lucky to survive the assault but was now realising just how close she and her son had come to death. She had in fact aimed at the droid's chest, but thankfully, her aim was poor.

"The female droid was not so plated, which is why the Duke was able to cut a big hole in her so easily. Had it been armoured…" Dr Schaffer trailed off. She was about to say, 'the Duke would not have been so lucky', but knew it was the wrong thing to say under the circumstances.

"Is there anything else you can tell me about the military droids?"

A knock at the door indicated Dr Schaffer's coffee was ready and she turned to take a steaming paper cup from a young man in military fatigues and an anxious demeanour, who glanced nervously at the Duchess before departing without a word. Dr Schaffer drank deeply from the paper coffee cup before replying, the aroma of fresh coffee filling the small room. "Hmm…yes...The droids were equipped with rifles of the heavy five hundred kilo volt variety capable of cutting through rock if need be and would cut through each of our shuttles out there like the proverbial hot knife through butter. The head units, as I said, are where the central processors are held, it's also where the communication components are held. In all three droids, the head and chest units were both lined with an isolated copper cage designed to redirect an electromagnetic pulse, like an internal Faraday Cage. I was hoping that would not be the case and if it were not, then potentially a single E.M.P. pulse would take out hundreds of these beastly bastards, but I'm afraid we will need to find some other way. The only weakness I was able to find is in the unarmoured neck. The abdomen is weak also but disconnecting the head from the body is more effective at stopping the beasts. So, directing fire at the neck may win some droid casualties but beyond that there is not much to tell. They are proficiently designed killing machines and difficult to destroy."

"What of the female droid."

"Ahh, now that is where I do have some good news," Mariam immediately felt her shoulders tense involuntarily, she did not want to trust to hope yet, for some way out of the inevitable doom they would all soon be facing. The scientist continued, "The female was an unarmoured, non-military droid, built to serve and provide pleasure and the like, she has the anatomy for it you see," she said flicking over images of the droid's lifelike naked body and female genitalia.

"I see."

"Yes, quite…men will be men, I suppose. Well, anyway, it appears this one's central circuits were still intact and were relaying information back to the shuttle in the square for local cache and forwarding onto Hydrax Prime. This droid, unlike the others, was fitted with an automated acid-based self-corruption mechanism, designed to destroy her core internal circuitry in the event of power failure, but it appears in the melee, the acid casing did not quite open as intended and only bored through the back of her head, doing no actual damage to the circuits themselves. That and the fact the Duke fired only at her chest, means the circuits are all intact.

"The droid stopped sending information when the power unit in her chest failed, but the shuttle continued to transmit all the data it had cached onto Hydrax Prime up until the moment the droid's transmission ended. When our men boarded the shuttle the communication conduit was then disconnected.

"The thing is, and I have to be cautious here, but it might, and I stress, it *might*, be possible for us to reopen the conduit using her circuitry and the Imperial shuttle as a relay. I would expect the central AI on Hydrax, should then authenticate the transmission automatically and we could then potentially have access to the Emperor's personal AI, in its entirety."

The Duchess was pleased, but cautious. "Okay. We would need to think about what we do if we did manage to get this doorway open."

"Well. I wouldn't expect it to be open for very long. I'm sure the AI is not so daft as to ignore the obvious question as to why one of its droids is suddenly back online, and it will probably attempt to sever the connection from its side, but a small window may be enough to slip something in. Something like a virus or worm."

"Can you do that?"

"I have a team of nerds barèly older than teens, but they have fairly good programming skills and I'm sure between us we can whip up something clever to corrupt the AI's central circuits. I would need to examine your own Cyrus. I believe it's built from the same tech and therefore probably shares much of the same basic architecture. The other thing, is that the AI is probably able to self-repair, so once it has identified the bug and eliminated it, it could probably restore itself from a backup version to repair any damage we do, but that would take time and could give us a longer window in which it would be offline and I would expect therefore, lose central control of its minions."

"That's great! Please proceed but we will need coordinate the viral attack as best we can to get the most advantage in whatever limited time window we have. You have my leave to examine Cyrus but please don't damage him, I need him."

"Surely, will do, ma'am. And may I say how sorry we all are about your husband you have my condolences."

"Thank you, Dr Schaffer." As the Duchess was taking her leave, Nobuhide hurriedly entered the meeting room almost bumping into the Duchess at the door, his left arm was in a high sling with his left hand at his right collar.

"I'm sorry I wasn't able to get here sooner."

"Nobuhide. I'm glad you are feeling better. You look well." In fact, the Duchess thought he looked as if he had aged ten or more years with deep lines and puffy bags under his eyes. He looked gaunt and exhausted, but it would do no good to tell him so.

"Apologies, ma'am, the medication I am taking for the pain makes me overtired and I had trouble waking this morning, and dressing also, with this thing," he said wagging his left elbow to indicate the problematic sling.

"It's no problem...I need to get back. But Dr Schaffer, would you please bring Nobuhide up to speed on what we have discussed." Turning now to Nobuhide she said, "Please see me in my office when you have finished, we need to discuss battle plans. I will be there all afternoon." With that the Duchess turned and made her way out, thanking the doctor for the glimmer of a hope she had provided, as a smile crept across her full lips.

Nobuhide turned back to the scientist. "Doctor, I need to speak to you about the Alcubierre engines. I need to understand how they work...I have an idea."

Chapter 12

Ibrahim could hear the sound of a man talking when he awoke on the second day after his ordeal in the Jebel Aswad Mountains, but was unable to discern the words that were spoken. As he tried to lift his head, he immediately felt a hot knife stab his neck, but his head did not fall backwards into the pillows behind him, as he expected when he relaxed, and for some reason there were restraint straps across his chest and legs. Right now though, he didn't care and couldn't think. His mind screamed for only one thing: *WATER! WATER! WATER!* He didn't care about anything else, if he had been captured by the Mahdi or was a death's door, he couldn't care less. If Nobunaga had been killed, he would be sad later, but for now he didn't care at all.

Through a dim blue fog he could make out a ghostly figure of a man standing at the foot of his bed, dressed in the surgical scrubs. *At least I'm not dead yet*, Ibrahim thought. The man seemed to notice he was awake as Ibrahim tried to speak. But his voice was a thin croak barely audible even to himself, let alone anyone else. So, instead he gestured to his mouth with his hand gripping an imaginary cup and tipping imaginary water into his mouth. *Drinky-drinky,* he thought.

"We'll get you a drink, hang on," the man said. He seemed to float away, returning a moment later with a plastic bottle of dark red juice in hand, a striped disposable straw poking out from the top. The lid was sealed with foil and the straw poked up through the seal. Ibrahim looked at the bottle and could see the liquid within it had risen to the top of the bottle and there was clear air beneath a floating bubble of red liquid that looked so much like blood. *We're in space,* he knew.

Ibrahim took a long draught of the cool, sweet, berry juice, and felt its silky, sweetness, soothe the dry aching in his throat as cold fingers caressed his neck, and moved down his chest. The drink was quickly finished, and he soon felt his wits returning as the sugar reached his blood. He tossed the empty bottle to the man who was busy writing on a tablet computer and saw it float gentle across to him. The man plucked it from the air around him and looked at Ibrahim, who gestured again with his drinky-drinky, sign. After a few minutes another bottle of the same berry juice was brought to him, and Ibrahim drunk it down hungrily.

Seeing Ibrahim awake, Nobunaga floated into the cabin and came to rest beside him. "How are you feeling, my friend? You scared us all for a while."

"I've seen better days. My neck really hurts. What happened?" Ibrahim's voice was still barely a croaky whisper, but he managed to speak.

Nobunaga was about to speak when the doctor interrupted them. "Hey, let him rest, he needs to heal his vocal cords. You can chat to him, but *you* don't talk back, Okay?" he said looking at his patient. Ibrahim nodded and the doctor turned to float out of the room using handrails positioned on the walls to guide his weightless body through the cabin doors.

"Anyway. We met the team after they found you. Apparently, they found the Mahdi dead with your sword sticking out of him and you were almost dead too, but the Alsuwayreans sprayed something to stop the bleeding and started giving you fluids and stuff. Then they got you on a stretcher and were carrying you out when we heard them and followed them back in the main entrance of the cave. They airlifted you by shuttle off the mountainside and the rest of us climbed back down. They've done some surgery on your neck and right now we're heading back to Carthage."

"Aisha?" Ibrahim croaked, ignoring the doctor's instruction.

"When the Mahdi died, most of his men surrendered and the ones that didn't, got killed pretty quickly anyway. You basically helped end their war and everyone is saying you're a hero, especially Aisha…Duchess Aisha, I mean. They're here, by the way. I mean not *here*, here, but they're on one of the shuttles with us and heading back to Carthage. I think she means to support the war against the Emperor," Nobunaga was smiling broadly. Ibrahim winced as he pushed his head back onto the pillows and patted Nobunaga's hand, before closing his eyes to sleep. *Heading home*, he thought with relief.

He drifted in and out of sleep then and when he awoke next, he was lying on a trolley and his mother was holding his hand, tears welling in her eyes as she gently stroked his hair. Silently, she kissed his forehead before letting go of his hand and his trolley was loaded on to the back of an ambulance. He slept again and soon found himself in a hospital bed in a side room off the main ward. His mother, Nobunaga, and

Nobuhide were at his bedside, Nobuhide's left arm still held in a sling.

As he opened his eyes, the brothers took their leave of the Duchess and gave her time alone with her son. She hugged him carefully and kissed his forehead again as he sat himself up feeling a slight stabbing in his neck as he did so. "How are you feeling? Can you speak?"

"I can, but it hurts a bit. How are you?" he said with a croak, as he took her hand.

"I'm fine now that you're back. I was getting worried about you. I hadn't heard anything for days and then this afternoon I got a message saying you were on your way back with Duchess Aisha. I'm so pleased you're okay, I kept praying Allah would keep you safe, and you've done it, you brought the Alsuwayreans on board! It's not over yet, but at least this gives me some hope that we can survive this."

"What happens next?"

"Don't you worry about that, you need to rest, I'm taking care of it all, you've done enough."

"I feel okay, just some pain in my neck but my voice is already getting better, I can tell, and I feel stronger."

"Okay just rest, I'll be back soon. Just keep sleeping, that will help you heal." She kissed his forehead again and swept out of the room, carrying his weapons. Ibrahim eased himself back down and felt at the thick bandage around his neck. Some soup was brought for him, and he slowly ate it, pleased that his injuries were not more severe and grateful that his limbs and faculties were all still intact.

Later that evening he swung his legs out of bed and slowly crossed the room in slippers to a wardrobe across from his bed. He had an intravenous catheter on the inside of his left elbow and a bandage around his neck and another on his left thigh. He wore only a hospital gown, open at the back, which he was keen to be out of. He pulled out some clothes his mother must have brought for him and dressed carefully taking care not to disturb his bandages as he pulled the clothes on. Feeling much better, he organised his hair as best he could, using a mirror above a basin and wet fingers to smooth out his unkempt curls. He then washed his face, dried himself with paper towels, and sat back on the edge of the bed, slightly tired from the exertion, but feeling altogether much stronger. He pulled on his trainers and made his way out of the room to the nurse's station. In a whisper he informed the nurse that he was self-discharging and signed some perfunctory paperwork before asked them to remove the cannula in his arm and arrange transport to take him back home.

It was night by the time he arrived home, the sky a dark blue, illuminated by a pale moon and the river of stars that ran across the sky from north to south, a billion fires in the distant heavens speaking of the vastness of the universe in which their colony was nothing more than an insignificant grain of sand.

As he entered the main reception room, he saw that except for the scorch marks which still blackened the walls, the earlier devastation had all but been erased. New furniture replaced that which had been the destroyed and the surviving tables, bookcases, and books all returned to the original places. A maid informed him Duchess Mariam was with Master Nobuhide and Duchess Aisha in the Duke's tower and he slowly made his way up the coiling staircase to see them.

He gave a light knock on the conference room door as he pushed it open and saw Duchess Aisha, General Faisal,

Nobuhide and his mother seated around the mahogany table with the black microphone to Cyrus in the centre. All stood immediately as he entered and began fussing over him.

"The hero of the hour! Welcome, Ibrahim, you look well," Duchess Aisha exclaimed as he entered.

"What are you doing here? You were supposed to be in the hospital for another night at least," his mother's voice was full of concern.

"Thank you," Ibrahim replied to the Duchess of Alsuwayra. "I'm fine, I need to be here," he said to his mother, his voice was becoming stronger now, but the wound on his neck still throbbed.

"You have done well, son. I have to admit I didn't think you and your friend would do much, but you proved me wrong, you got him…," General Faisal said in his familiar gruff tone.

"And helped end the war on our colony. Well done," Duchess Aisha finished for him.

"Thank you. I just did what I'm sure anyone else would have done. But please don't let me interrupt, we have a war to plan."

"Indeed, we were just getting started in fact," Nobuhide said. At Duchess Mariam's instruction he continued, looking down intermittently at some papers before him, as he spoke "General Faisal and Duchess Aisha have informed us the Mahdi terrorist that you killed was being financed by the Emperor."

"Yes. When we examined the computers and documents in his cave, we found evidence of money transfers from Hydrax Prime. It seems the Emperor wanted to stir up trouble on Alsuwayra to keep us out of Duke's Hazahari's alliance.

That is why we have decided it is necessary for us to join this fight," Duchess Aisha said. "But please, Master Nobuhide, continue."

'He has his uses,' Ibrahim remembered the Mahdi saying of the Emperor.

"Okay, we know the Emperor is sending his fleet, but we don't know precisely when or where they will arrive. We suspect their ships will drop out of their Alcubierre distortions around three to four thousand kilometres from the planet's surface, as that is standard operating procedure for interplanetary travel, and we can estimate where roughly they will be in relation to the planet when they do, but the key thing is we don't know when they will arrive. But…I have been working on a plan with Dr Schaffer and we might be able to have something waiting for them when they arrive."

"What is it?" Faisal asked.

Nobuhide was about to explain when Dr Schaffer suddenly burst into the room, breathless from running up the long tower staircase, her eyes were wide and looking larger than usual behind her thick lenses. "Don't say another word!" she shouted, panting for breath, her hair a dishevelled tangle of grey and black, her forehead shiny with sweat. She took them all by surprise and General Faisal reached immediately for the weapon at his hip and made to stand, but Mariam saw his movement and raised her palm to indicate for him to stop.

"What is it Dr Schaffer?" she asked, afraid the Imperial fleet had already arrived.

"We can't talk here, please come outside."

"We can all speak here. We are all allies and friends."

"No! I *must* speak to you outside. Please!"

Mariam rose and apologised to the Alsuwayreans, confused by Dr Schaffer's odd behaviour. Outside, Dr Schaffer led the Duchess back into the stairwell of the tower. *Has she lost her mind? Does she mean to throw me down the stairs?* the Duchess wondered.

"Sorry, Duchess, I need to speak with you away from Cyrus. Do you have your phone with you?" she asked, still panting.

"No, it's in the conference room, why what's happened?"

"Okay, good. You let me examine Cyrus to determine vulnerabilities in his software architecture and I was looking at his subroutine processes to understand how he handles communications dataflow, but I couldn't understand why all the data was being copied to his communication buffer and re-routed back to the Hypernet Nebula and then I checked, and I found the software and so I examined him further and I found the hardware, wired in."

"Sorry, Dr Schaffer, I don't follow. Please, speak to me plainly."

"Cyrus has been hacked. I got the security feeds from the server room. They are on a separate feed from the main system precisely to prevent this type of thing." As she spoke the scientist displayed images of the server room on her tablet computer. "Six weeks ago, this man put a device in the server room and connected it up to Cyrus' servers. It's still there I didn't want to remove it without speaking to you first. Basically, it's been copying and relaying all of Cyrus' sensor information and communication data to the Hypernet Nebula and then onto Hydrax Prime. It could also be manipulating Cyrus' sensors." The images showed a man in a shirt and trousers, bending over the computer hardware in the server room, his back to the camera. As the man straightened and turned to his left, his features were unmistakable, the Duchess recognised him at once…Zaid Abbas, her one-time lover.

The Duchess felt as if the scientist had just punched her in the stomach, she felt lightheaded, her legs gave way under her and she slumped against the wall of the stairwell on her haunches, her palms together, her head resting on her wrists. *Oh god*, she thought. *They know everything, all our plans, our secrets everything. They're too far ahead of us. We've already lost it all.* Ibrahim and Nobuhide rushed into the stairwell then and looked suspiciously at Dr Schaffer and down at the Duchess sitting on her haunches, tears welling in her eyes. Ibrahim squatted down next to her, and she reached out and stroked his hair from his face. *It was all for nothing*, she thought. Ibrahim turned from her and stared back at the scientist, still standing with her tablet computer in hand.

"Dr Schaffer, what is going on, what is happening?" he demanded, his voice croaking.

"Sorry, I couldn't speak in there. Do you have your phones with you?"

"Yes, you need to call someone?" Ibrahim asked, handing the smooth rectangle of glass to the scientist as Nobuhide pulled out his phone. Dr Schaffer took both the phones, opened the door to the stairwell and slid them across the floor, closing the door behind them.

Both men gaped at her in confusion, but before they could ask what she was doing, she answered them: "Cyrus has been hacked. Everything…every email, every conversation we have in his presence is being recorded and copied and sent to Hydrax Prime, for the last six weeks. Maybe even every telephone conversation we have between each other as well, but I'm not sure about that. But basically, it means Hydrax Prime know everything."

"Our troops, our defences, our plans for evacuation?" Ibrahim asked, though he knew the answer.

"Basically. If it was ever discussed in front of Cyrus, it is probably known to the Emperor."

The Duchess thought of Zaid and her last conversation with him, they had argued over Ibrahim. *If that got out it would destroy her son. I have to tell him about the lie, the hideous lie, before he finds out from someone else. I have to tell him that Ichiro knew. He helped me…he forgave me.* She slowly lifted herself off her haunches and took a deep breath. "Shut Cyrus down, I don't want him listening in on our conversations any longer."

"Duchess, with respect, all is not lost. This could be a blessing in disguise. We could use this to our advantage," Dr Schaffer continued. "Depending on what you have already spoken of regarding battle plans, we could use this. The Emperor thinks we don't know about the hack, so we continue to pretend as if we don't know anything and we misdirect him, send his forces somewhere where we can have the advantage."

"Yes!" Nobuhide said. "We can make out as if we are building a defensive base on the moon and get them to assemble there, then we can open up the black hole, we talked about and suck them all in a destroy them."

"Black hole? *What?*" Ibrahim asked, puzzled.

"We don't know if that would work Nobu, it's all highly theoretical…and dangerous," Dr Schaffer replied.

The Duchess stood now, regaining her composure. "We can't talk here like this. Let's move somewhere where we can talk and get Aisha and Faisal up to speed. Where is safe?" she asked looking at Schaffer.

"I can sweep the Duke's office for communication devices, give me a few minutes."

They all left the stairwell and both Ibrahim and Nobuhide collected their phones from the floor and returned to the conference room where Duchess Aisha and General Faisal were growing impatient.

"What is going on? What's happened?" General Faisal demanded gruffly.

"Dr Schaffer is not well, I'm afraid. I think the stress has got to her. I need to take care of something just now, but please let's meet again in twenty minutes in the Duke's office next door. I won't be long.", the Duchess said looking at the microphone that was Cyrus' ear in the room. She and the other Carthagians left the room after leaving their phones on the conference room table. The General was not pleased at the delay, but Duchess Aisha put a gentle restraining hand on his forearm.

Chapter 13

Twenty minutes later, the small war council convened in the late Duke's office as Dr Schaffer carried a collection of earpieces, capable of communicating with Cyrus, to the conference room, where General Faisal and Duchess Aisha had left their phones at Mariam's instruction. Nobuhide pulled some chairs in from the conference room and all six sat around the Duke's desk knee to knee, with the Duchess taking the Duke's desk chair. A light film of dust covered the papers and maps strewn across the desk and Duchess Mariam pushed them aside to clear the space, kicking up a small cloud of dust motes as he did so.

She explained how Cyrus had been compromised and how they intended to use this as means of misdirecting the Emperor. A plan to which they all concurred. Mariam also explained how they planned to infect the Emperor's AI with a virus, using the Alexion droid and the Imperial shuttle. "General, how many forces can Alsuwayra muster for this fight?" she asked.

"I have ordered a skeleton defence crew to remain on Alsuwayra and the rest of the force is already on its way. That's two hundred and ninety fighter craft armed with plasma cannons and two large transport ships, capable of transporting ten thousand passengers each. I expect them here in the next…two hours and fifty minutes," the General replied, glancing down at his watch which was still on Alsuwayra time.

"We have also reached out to Stanislaw Soccoli on Vega-3 and Stephen Wang on Sino-Axiom Prime. Both were party to the planned alliance and wanted to support it, but I am yet to hear back from them. I was going to ask Cyrus to link up with our systems on Alsuwayra so I can check for a response, but now that is out of the question," Aisha added.

"Ma'am, I would suggest that we send a scout ship out to Hydrax Prime. None of the information we have at present can be relied upon as all of it has been conveyed to us by Cyrus and may therefore have been subject to interference from Hydrax. We could be facing two hundred ships, or we could be facing two thousand, we need verification of the information that has been sent to us," Dr Schaffer suggested.

"Agreed. I will send a scout shuttle up for a quick look and get them to come straight back. Is your virus ready?" Mariam asked the scientist.

"Yes, I think it is. I have not tested it, but I am quite confident it will work. I would have liked to have tested it, but it will serve, I am sure."

Quite confident is not very reassuring, Mariam thought, but she asked, "How much time will it give us?"

"Once the gateway to the AI is open, the transfer of the virus will take approximately ten minutes, it is a large file you see. Once the transfer is done, the virus will get to work unpackaging itself and corrupting the source code of the core communications functions first and then the quantum control units, which will take it offline within minutes and force it to reboot from a backup. After that it's a crapshoot as to how long the AI stays offline before it recovers. I simply cannot say how long that will be, I'm afraid. If it were Cyrus I would estimate probably an hour, so if the Alexion system is more advanced, as I suspect it is, you are looking at less than that, in which to do as much damage as possible to the hardware they're sending."

"Ten minutes is far too long, surely the AI will sever the connection in that time," Faisal said.

"That is a risk. I wanted to route the shuttle's communications through Cyrus, so he could boost the signal through the Hypernet Nebula and speed everything up, but now that Cyrus has been compromised, I don't want to risk that. So, it would need to be done from the ground here."

"What if you flew the shuttle to Hydrax Prime and did the hack locally from there?" Ibrahim suggested.

"Yes, that would work as long as the droid and the necessary software were on board. The long latency of attempting a large file transfer over such profound distances is the key issue, so cutting the distance will get the speed down to a second or less. I did consider that, but the issue is the associated risk. As soon as the AI detects the intrusion, the shuttle would become the target of a massive military manhunt."

"I'll do it," Ibrahim had no real reason to believe he could get out alive, but his first taste of battle against the Mahdi had embolden him. He had the growing feeling that he knew what his role in the grand design, Imam Omar spoke of, was now going to be. *Why else would Allah have spared me, if not to have a critical role in turning the tide of this war*, he thought.

"You won't. It's too dangerous. Dr Schaffer is right, it's a suicide mission," Mariam countered.

"I can do it. I need to do it. To avenge my father."

The Duchess winced at the word. She knew she had to tell him before he threw his life away for a lie. Before she could respond however, Ibrahim continued, turning to Nobuhide as he spoke. "What was this black hole plan, you were talking about?"

"So, the Alcubierre engines all create a small naked singularity at the front of a shuttle by emitting a stream of graviton particles. The singularity folds spacetime and shortens the physical distance between two points. The engines then dissipate the fold at their rear using a stream of anti-graviton particles. This basically contracts spacetime at the front and expands it at the rear of the shuttles. That's right, isn't it doc?"

"More or less. You've got the general gist of it," Dr Schafer confirmed, not wanting to get into the technical detail of Casimir vacuums, shearing forces, and the quantum spin of negative mass particles.

"So, if we can get six shuttles together in perpendicular planes and all firing their Alcubierre engines at the same spot, we can in theory open up a self-sustaining black hole. If we continue firing for a few minutes after the black hole is created, the hole would become large enough to consume the enemy craft."

"And the shuttles!" Aisha exclaimed.

"That's one of the risks, but they would not need to be manned shuttles of course if we have Cyrus at our disposal. Even if you could get it to work, and in theory it would, you would struggle to close it again using the anti-graviton field the Alcubierre engines generate at their rear because its mass will be augmented by whatever it draws in. It's too risky in my opinion." Dr Schaffer doused Nobuhide's enthusiasm for the idea. He wanted a swift end to the war with minimal engagement and this, in his opinion would be best way of achieving that aim.

"Let's park that idea and use it if all else fails. Cyrus can launch the shuttles remotely and begin firing, before the Emperor's forces can respond, even if they become aware of what we are doing. But I don't relish the idea of creating a black hole in the vicinity of our planet. The whole point is to try to survive this war, not create a new way of killing us all," Duchess Mariam ended the discussion on that front.

"So, in summary, I will send up a scout ship and review who to send with Dr Schaffer on the hacking run to Hydrax"

"Wait, *I'm* going?" Dr Schaffer was surprised.

"Is there anyone else better equipped to get it done?" Mariam asked the scientist.

"I suppose. Fair enough," Dr Schaffer looked down at the desk, the prospect of flying into a hornet's nest full of automated drones, to kill the queen hornet, did not enthuse her as it seemed to do for Ibrahim.

"Once our forces arrive, I suggest we begin evacuation to Alsuwayra at once and establish a perimeter of shuttles in orbit at a distance of three thousand kilometres. They will arrive without warning, and we therefore need to be up and ready not sitting on the ground," General Faisal instructed.

"Agreed. If we are ready then, we will need to perform a little farce for Cyrus," Mariam said.

They returned to the conference room and began outlining their fake plan for Cyrus' benefit. They spoke of forming a base of Alsuwayrean shuttles on the Carthagian moon and from there they would assault the Imperial Fleet as they dropped out of their spacetime distortions to take up formation around the planet. The only truth they spoke of, was that Dr Schaffer had succeeded in retrofitting plasma cannons to each of the eleven Carthagian shuttles at their disposal.

They concluded their faux plan and made their way back into the Duke's office to speak again.

"Dr Schaffer, now that that is done. Please see to restoring Cyrus as soon as you can, we will need him online when the Imperial Fleet arrives. He is our eyes and ears in space until we get a scout ship up."

Yes. He'll be offline for a few minutes but hopefully I'll get him back up and running without any problems. Once that's done, I suggest that I get the Alexion hack ready on the Imperial shuttle.

"Yes, have it ready so we can use it at a moment's notice. You will need to be in orbit around Hydrax Prime. Please take one of the pilots from the Eastern Base and depart when you are ready.

"Ibrahim. Please stay with Dr Schaffer and see that she has everything she needs. But I don't want you going to Hydrax, I need you here to assist with the evacuation."

Their phones in the conference room all began to ring then in a mad cacophony of mixed-up jingles, overlaid by a loud bleeping alarm coming from Cyrus's speaker in the room. They all rushed back into the room.

"Cyrus what's happened? What's the matter?" the Duchess asked, though she already knew the answer.

"Apologies for the alarm sound ma'am, I have been unable to reach you. The Imperial forces have just appeared on my sensors and have begun to assemble at a distance of two thousand kilometres from the planet's surface."

"They're here," Mariam whispered.

"Yes. So far one hundred and fifty Imperial fighters are…"

"Cyrus?…Cyrus?" the Duchess quickly picked up an earpiece and began tapping it to raise her synthetic intelligence, but there was no response. Cyrus was offline and the war they had knew was coming, had finally arrived.

Chapter 14

Zaid Abbas drove slowly on the unpaved gravel road that led up to the main gate of Northern quarry and lowered his window to speak to the lone security guard sitting in his booth next to the gate. The guard was a young man, perhaps in his early twenties with thin, floppy, yellow hair, and a bright red pimple in the fold of skin at his left nostril. He was in the middle of watching something on the small screen of his telephone. Before Zaid could utter a word, the guard spoke in tone thick with boredom: "Quarry's closed...no visitors allowed." his eyes never straying from his device.

"I'm Dr Zaid Abbas, I'm a member of the Privy Council. Open up please."

"Quarry's closed... no one allowed in," the guard repeated.

"I'm here on official business, the Duchess has asked me to take a look at the cave they found, there's some health and safety issues I need to check on."

"No-one told me nothing about no health and safety issues."

"I'm sorry, they should have done. Who's your manager? I will see they are punished for not passing the message along." *Most of these asses, harbour deep resentment for their superiors and using this approach is like leading them with a nice juicy carrot*, Zaid mused.

"Who'd you say you were?" the guard was looking at him now and inspecting him and his shiny black car, lightly dusted with sand.

"Dr Zaid Abbas, I am the Chef Medical Officer of Carthage," he replied, flashing the guard his hospital identification badge.

"Fine, fine, here you go, sign in," he said, passing him a large visitor's logbook and pen. Zaid duly signed the book and returned it through the guard's window before asking: "Where is the new cave they found, the one that's causing all the fuss?"

"Go straight to the end of this road and you will see it with a *No Entry* sign. There is a ladder you can use to get down to it, next to the cave entrance. You can't miss it."

Zaid got underway and sped down the stony road as soon as the gates were opened. Signing into the logbook would reveal his identity, of course, but he didn't plan to wait around to be caught. He would take whatever this artefact was and then get over to Hydrax Prime as soon as he could. Stealing a shuttle would be trickier than getting access to the quarry no doubt, but he would worry about that later. For now, he wanted to get the pictures and send them, so he could get paid. Alistair Jamieson had proven himself reliable in that respect at least and *if he was willing to pay five hundred and fifty thousand New Dollars for pictures, he would be willing to pay a lot more for the real thing.*

Zaid soon found himself at the cave entrance as the guard had described, a small red metal fence had been placed around a metre-wide hole in the ground with the words '*No Entry*' painted across the fence in large white letters. Next to it was a plastic chest of equipment. Peering down into the hole with the torch of his phone he could see the floor of the cave, quite some distance down. A small ladder lay beside the fence but at three metres in length, it was far too short to reach the cavern floor. He searched the contents of the chest and found a harness, a pair of gloves, a hardhat and a long metal cable which would usually be attached to a winch of some kind. But there was no such winch in the chest, and he was loth to go back to the dim-witted security guard for help. Looking around he came up with a solution. Donning the gloves but ignoring the hard-hat, he slowly and laboriously tied the metal cable as best he could into a slip knot and slid its large adjustable loop over the rear wheel of his car. Then moving the car forward slightly, he managed to thread the loop around the wheel of his car. *That would support my weight surely*, he thought. He threw the other end down into the cave and gathered his gym bag from the boot of his car. He emptied its contents into the boot and slung the empty bag across his back so he could use his hands. He began lowering himself into the cave, hanging onto the rope with his gloved hands, his black leather shoes scraping against the wall of the drill shaft.

After a long slow descent, he entered the cave from above and found to his dismay that the cable was at least two metres too short. He was about to drop down to the cave floor but realised it would be impossible for him to get back out, so instead he slowly heaved himself back up and out of the drill shaft. When he got back to the top, he dragged himself over the edge of the shaft and lay on his back panting, his arms ached from the exertion and his shirt was sodden with sweat and now caked in dust.

He was thinking for a while, then found a solution. He knotted the harness he had found to the top rung of the ladder and clipped it to the end of his metal cable. He then slowly lowered the ladder down the shaft until he felt it touch the floor of the cave and began his descent again. This time when he reached the end of the cable, he clambered down onto the ladder that was dangled awkwardly from the cable. But it served. He carefully climbed down the hanging ladder which swung from side to side under his weight as the harness slipped from side to side, on the rung it was knotted to. Once down on the cavern floor, he gathered some rocks to anchor the feet of the ladder as best he could to try to stabilise it.

He used his flashlight of his phone to search the cave and could see little of interest at first, then in the centre of the cave he saw the cairn. A pile of red-brown rocks a metre high and two metres long, which clearly looked like a grave. The dead however did not frighten the doctor and he moved to the cairn to take a closer look. On it he saw a rectangular slab with the curious markings, but these meant nothing to him, and he pushed the slab aside without a further thought. Looking into the cairn he saw beneath the slab, a glass cube, within which was an apple. He picked up the box and examined it carefully, turning it over in his hands repeatedly. The apple had a reddish-gold colour and sat on a small cushion of green silk but rolled around inside the box when he turned it. He could see a bite had been taken out of the apple, but in the light of his phone, the flesh inside looked healthy enough. The edges of the cube were sealed tight against one another, but he thought he could probably pry them open with a knife, if he had one, or failing that, he could smash it open on a rock. *This is what all the fuss is about? A half-eaten apple. What a joke!*

This is NOT an alien artefact! He set the box to one side and searched the rest of the cairn, but it was completely empty, no sign of anything else and no bones, human, animal or otherwise. He took his phone and swung its light around the rest of the cave. '*Hopefully, you'll know it when you see it*', Alistair had said, but right now he couldn't be sure this apple was the artefact the Emperor had been searching for. *Maybe this is some practical joke Alistair has setup?* he thought, *but then he wouldn't have sent even half of the money. But what if it's a trap? Maybe they want to catch me in the act?* Zaid whirled around at the thought and moved to the ladder, standing in silence at its feet and craning his neck to look up into the drill shaft. He listened for sounds of security guards or the local police force, and looked for the light of their sirens, but there was nothing, only the ghostly howling of the wind as it blew down the drill shaft, whistling and moaning to him as it blew.

He didn't understand. He slumped against a rock and looked again at the glass box thinking. *Why would Ichiro shut down the mine for this, an apple? This must be more significant than it looks*, he thought. The only significant apple he could think of though was the forbidden fruit of Paradise. According to the religion he only nominally followed, the forbidden fruit had transformed Adam and Eve from vague spiritual beings into defined male and female forms and which resulted in them to be cast down to Earth as a punishment for their disobedience. *This couldn't be…No way…This is a hoax, it has to be. The Qur'an doesn't say it was an apple anyway, does it? That was from the Bible, wasn't it?*

Zaid had never had much faith in Islam or any other religion for that matter. The idea of some mystical being creating people just to send them to Hell if they couldn't withstand the natural inclinations, God had endowed them with, or sending them to Heaven if they were good little Muslims, lived like monks, and prayed five times day. That just seemed unfair to him. It was just too fantastical to believe in a great Heaven beyond the stars or some great Hell either. To Zaid, religion was just another system of control that brainwashed people into voluntarily submitting its dogmatic restrictions. *But, if this is the forbidden fruit, then…that means…No it can't be, this has to be a hoax…But…what if it is? Maybe I should ask forgiveness for my sins. Just in case.*

He was considering making a prayer in the cave, then and there, when greed and the memory of his promised riches, restored him to his senses. He stood up, shook his head as if to shake off the silly idea, and collected his bag, He took photos of the tablet and the glass box with his phone but, with no network connection this far underground, he was unable to send the images to Alistair. So he lifted the inscribed tablet into the bag he had brought and then carefully placed the glass box on top. He zipped the bag shut and slung it over his shoulder, feeling the weight of it dig into his shoulder as he did so, then he slowly made his way back to the surface, the muscles of his arms screaming at him in pain as he slowly pulled himself up.

Back at the surface, Zaid tried to send the images he had taken to Alistair, but the network was oddly down, and he was unable to get a signal. He freed the metal cable from his car's wheel and clambered back into it, placing his bag on the passenger seat. As he drove away from the quarry's main gate, he turned his car towards the Eastern Military Base and pushed his car as fast as he dared on the unpaved gravel road. *Now onto stage two*, he thought.

Chapter 15

In the Duke's conference room, panic was surging as everyone spoke hurriedly over each other. Without Cyrus, the ability of the Carthagian forces to communicate and coordinate amongst themselves had been reduced to sending hand-delivered messages. In one swoop, their entire defensive plans were in disarray. Mariam could feel the anxiety in the air, so she took control. *It is my colony to defend and so I must rise to this challenge*, she thought. "Dr Schaffer, we need this hack done *now*. You need to get going."

"Yes, I'll get Cyrus up and running first and then get underway."

"If you get Cyrus up and running, could you do the hack from here?" Mariam asked.

Dr Schaffer thought for a moment, then replied. "I could, but I'm not sure what has been downloaded to Cyrus' mainframe so now that I know he has been compromised, I wouldn't trust him fully until I've done a full diagnostic scan and that would take at least twelve hours. Doing it independently of Cyrus from orbit around Hydrax is still the surest way."

"Okay, please make it so." Turning to her Alsuwayrean allies now, Mariam continued, "General Faisal, how long now until the Alsuwayrean force is here?"

"They should be here in the next two and half hours." He glanced at his watch as he replied.

"Okay, Nobuhide, go straight to the Eastern Military Base and get our shuttles up. We need them up and fighting. We have ambulances, mining trucks and cars. Let's start getting everyone we can to the caves as soon as we can." She dialled number after number on her phone but there was no signal. No-one she could reach. "Ibrahim, stay with Dr Schaffer make sure she's safe. But under no circumstances, go to Hydrax Prime, I need you here."

"Understood," he replied knowing he would disobey her. He knew he shouldn't, in the midst of this crisis, but the need to be out in front with the others risking their lives was too great for him to simply ignore. He knew he had a role to play in this grand design.

The Duchess darted out of the room and raced down the steps of the tower, thinking about how to get the evacuation started. They had assumed they would have telephone capabilities and Cyrus at least. No-one had anticipated a scenario where Cyrus was unavailable to them. The infantile hubris of their dismal preparations stung at her.

Dr Schaffer and Ibrahim were soon racing behind the Duchess as they descended the stairs heading for the basement of the ducal residence, where Cyrus' core servers were secured. When they got to the bottom of the stairwell, they turned right through a door that opened to a short staircase that led them into the main reception room. They crossed the room and opened another door to yet another staircase that took them much further down into the basement, which Ibrahim knew was heavily fortified. Once there, Dr Schaffer swiped her identification pass at the door lock and a two foot wide metal door with steel reinforcement, swung slowly open towards them. "It was wise that the server room security was not tied to the AI, like the rest of the residence, exactly for this scenario. Otherwise an intruder who gained control of the AI could lock everyone out." she said as they passed the doors.

Inside the server room, a desk was fitted with a small unlit computer display, keyboard, and next to it a small microphone and speaker, similar to that kept in the Duke's conference room in the tower above. Beyond the desk, numerous shelves were stacked with sleek black rectangular boxes all connected together with insulated fibre optic cables. *Server arrays*, Ibrahim knew. Each of the servers had LED display panels but none of them were lit. Beyond the shelving, four large gold cylinders, each almost a foot in diameter and reaching almost to the ceiling, were bathed in a tank of blue liquid in the centre of the room, on the outside of which, beads of condensation were running down into a drain built into the floor. Cables connected the tops of the cylinders to the server arrays. "That's where the magic happens," Dr Schaffer explained, indicating the gold cylinders.

She moved behind the server arrays and rooted around behind them for a while before emerging clutching a sleek black rectangular device with cables protruding from one side. She then moved behind the cylindrical tubing and its tank of fluid, to power units lined against the wall and began checking them, holding the small black unit the size of a telephone, in her hand. Once satisfied that the power units were intact and functional, she returned to the keyboard and display unit and dumped the device on the desk as she seated herself into a swivel chair, the only seat in the room. Ibrahim stood next to her, unable to assist, but ready to follow her instructions. She typed furiously into the keyboard and looked up repeatedly at the monitor in front of her. After five or so minutes, a white chevron appeared on the screen, and she knew she had finally gained access. She continued typing lines of code until eventually, the display turned a dark blue and a large white dot appeared in the centre of the display which throbbed in time with Cyrus' voice. "Good Evening Dr Schaffer. How are you today?" Cyrus' familiar voice came through the speaker beside the keyboard loud and clear. In that moment, neither Ibrahim nor Dr Schaffer thought they had ever heard a sweeter voice. They both let out a deep sigh of relief.

Dr Schaffer explained in technical terms to Cyrus why he had been offline and checked with him that communications had been restored and that his sensors had detected the Imperial Fleet in orbit around their planet. She would have preferred to do a full diagnostic scan but there was not enough time. She dialled Duchess Mariam on her phone to inform her of the good news.

Duchess Mariam was at the mosque speaking with Imam Omar. At her instruction, he had ordered an impromptu call to prayer to signal that all was not well and as the believers began arriving to investigate, he outlined what was happening and the need to evacuate to the caves. Several boys and teenagers were sent to run from house to house to tell everyone to come to the mosque. Her phone rang then, and she knew instantly that Cyrus was back online.

"Duchess. Cyrus is back online and appears to be functioning normally."

"Great work, doctor. Can you please ask Cyrus to send an Emergency Evacuation Order to all phones connected to the mobile network. The message should tell everyone to make their way to the Kirishima Caves if they have transport, but if they are unable to travel, to make their way to the Grand Mosque. Also, ask Cyrus to contact the police. I want that bastard Zaid Abbas, arrested as soon as possible."

"Right oh, will do. Once we do that Ibrahim and I will make our way to the Eastern Military Base and get started on the hack."

"Got it, thanks."

A minute later, Mariam's phone and those of everyone else in the mosque began blaring to the sound of an Emergency Notice. The message transmitted in text form exactly as she had instructed. Mariam checked her watch, *still two hours and ten minutes until the Alsuwayreans arrive*, she thought. She turned back to the small crowd of people in the mosque's main prayer hall and asked for volunteers to drive people to the caves. Several men she did not know volunteered, which encouraged others to do the same. She instructed them to get to the Imperial Mine at the west of the city and to collect flatbed trucks and other any large vehicles they can find and bring them back to the mosque as quickly as they could. "As soon as you're back, get everyone on board the trucks as quickly as you can and head to the Kirishima caves. Take whatever you can carry but don't waste time. We don't know how long it will be before the bombs start falling."

Mariam then dialled the number for Cyrus and requested he put her through to the conference room where Duchess

Aisha and General Faisal would still be waiting. As he waited for a response in the conference room, Aisha and the General walked into the mosque.

"We heard the adhan and saw your Emergency broadcast, so we came here," General Faisal explained.

"Great, I was just trying to reach you. I don't know anywhere that is completely safe just now, but the caves may offer some protection, so we are evacuating everyone to there. Imam Omar can take you there as soon as he gets back from the Imperial mine. We are going to steal their trucks to move people to the caves," Mariam reported.

"Good thinking. Don't worry about us. I was a refugee from Syria in the conflict there thirty years ago, we will make it through this. I think its best we go to your military base. Our shuttle is there, so once our troops arrive, we will join them in orbit and start whacking these droids," Aisha said.

"I'm heading there now, let's go now then."

The two duchesses and the general made their way out and back to the ducal residence across the square and from there they rode in the duchess's car to the Eastern Military Base.

As Ibrahim and Dr Schaffer arrived at the base, they saw ten white Carthagian shuttles lifting off in quick succession. They made their way to the control room in the main building at the base and spoke with Colonel Jehangir Khan. He was a stout man in his fifties, with a long black, elaborately lacquered moustache that curled upwards at both ends and dropped over his upper lip. He had fought in the Great War on Earth and claimed to trace his ancestry to the Mughal Emperor Aurangzeb.

"We have nine of the shuttles in orbit and one that Dr Zaid has taken on his mission," Colonel Khan explained.

"Dr Zaid Abbas?" Ibrahim and Dr Schaffer looked at one another, stunned.

"Yes, he said the Duchess had a top-secret diplomatic mission for him and he was to travel to Hydrax Prime. He was very insistent, wouldn't listen to me at all. I was unable to contact anyone to check but he was saying it was a matter of life and death for the whole colony."

"Life and death for him, more like. He's a traitor. He's the reason Cyrus was disabled. If you see him again, kill him." Ibrahim instructed.

"Oh, I see. Certainly. Will do," Khan looked embarrassed at his faux pas as he saluted and turned away, but both Ibrahim and Dr Schaffer had sympathy for him. They would have probably done the same in his position.

"He could not have gone far, perhaps we can catch him with the Imperial Shuttle."

"He's not important let him go. We need to get the hack done before they can start their attack."

Ibrahim collected a plasma handgun and a dagger from the weapons store, and they quickly made their way to Dr Schaffer's office, where the Alexion droid was naked on a table with her chest cut open in the midline from the base of her neck to her groin. Cables protruded from her skull reached out like white medusan snakes to a number of laptop computers propped against her body. Dr Schaffer quickly disconnected the droid and Ibrahim swung its body over his shoulder, surprised by the heavy weight of it as he staggered out of the door, his neck wound pinching at him as he moved.

Dr Schaffer followed closely behind with one of her laptops clutched under her arm.

Together they made their way from the main building out to the landing strip where two Carthagian shuttles sat alongside the Alsuwayrean shuttle, in which Duchess Aisha had arrived, and the Imperial shuttle that had brought the droids to kill the Duke. Men were climbing into the sleek rectangular Carthagian shuttles and Ibrahim could see both vessels had been fitted with large grey plasma cannons just aft of the long cylindrical Alcubierre engines that sat on the backs of their fuselages. Dr Schaffer and Ibrahim climbed up the ramp of the grey and black Imperial Shuttle and Ibrahim dropped the naked droid into a chair behind the pilot's station.

The interior of the Imperial vessel was much like the Carthagian shuttles in design, having all been manufactured on Hydrax Prime by the same corporation and Ibrahim was able to quickly familiarise himself with the controls. The main difference he noted was that the Imperial vessel had already been armed with a plasma cannon and was heavily adorned with gold. The dashboard between the buttons and lights, the pillars supporting the front window, as well as the entire ceiling, were all gilded. *Probably paint*, he thought, as real gold would make the craft much heavier to fly. "This Emperor is fond of his gold, isn't he?" Ibrahim remarked.

"Apparently, he covers himself in it. From head to toe."

"Really? That's weird..."

"Hey, you're not supposed to be coming, what are you doing?"

"My mother told me to keep you safe, so that's what I intend to do." Dr Schaffer did not argue, it was between mother and son, but in any case, she would prefer to have some company for such a dangerous mission. The thought of dying alone in space had not especially enthused her when the Duchess had volunteered her for this mission.

Ibrahim powered up the shuttle's jets and closed the ramp, slowly lifting them off form the landing strip below. Dr Schaffer meanwhile strapped herself to a seat alongside the droid and began connecting the cables still dangling from its head to the laptop she carried. They were soon airborne and hovering over the tarmac. As began their ascent to space, the proximity sensors on board began to bleep rapidly. As they hurriedly tried to discern the threat, the four storey building behind them, exploded into flame and buffeted their vessel, causing it to be thrown across the tarmac, the end of its right wing scrapping on the ground, as Ibrahim corrected the movement with his jets. He swung the craft around to face the building which they saw, to their horror, had now suddenly been reduced to a pile of burning rubble, flames whirling up to the night sky above.

"We have to go, NOW!" Schaffer shouted. The quaver in her voice betraying the fear she felt. Ibrahim lifted the craft and fired the jets, pressing them back into their seats, and taking them up and away from the runway as more missiles rained down on the base. The shuttles still on the tarmac exploded below them as another missile slammed into the ground where they had sat a few moments ago, ripping open the tarmac to leave behind a deep crater in the rock and sand beneath.

The shuttle was soon in space and around them they could see hundreds of Imperial vessels in long rows stretching out into the distance. The vessels were evenly spaced almost midway between the planet and its moon, and they were all facing the planet's northern pole. Every few seconds a shuttle would break formation to swoop down towards the planet's surface. Dr Schaffer tapped on a keyboard on the dashboard looking up at a holographic screen projected before her. "Good, the shuttle is sending out a beacon signal indicating we are an Imperial vessel, so we shouldn't be harassed by any of this lot."

Ibrahim was about to reply, but in the distance, to their starboard side, he could see three separate dogfights occurring with some of the Carthagian shuttles that had departed earlier. They darted and dived in elaborate coils trying their best to evade volley after volley shot from a hoard of Imperial Fighters that were forming loose spheres around each of the Carthagian shuttles. He reached for the controls of the plasma cannon, but Dr Schaffer grabbed his wrist. "Our mission is too important. We must not be noticed," she instructed.

Ibrahim quickly manoeuvred their stolen shuttle into empty space away from the Imperial troops and pulled up schematics from the Imperial shuttle's computer which provided the navigation they needed to journey to Hydrax Prime. The onboard computer plotted their route to Hydrax Prime and Ibrahim immediately initiated the sequence to get underway. They were quickly enveloped in the pale blue light of the distorted spacetime around them and swept away.

Chapter 16

As Duchess Mariam approached the Eastern Military Base in her car with Duchess Aisha and General Faisal, a volley of rockets whistled down to slam into the main building at the base. The explosion was so bright, the black of night became day for a long moment as bright yellow and red flame billowed out across the base like rolling clouds. A shockwave of air buffeted the car and the building collapsed almost instantly with a thunderous rumble that shook the ground and continued for what felt like several minutes as flames and dust leapt up to the dome of the dark sky above. Mariam stopped her car and jumped out, her other passengers also exiting to stand looking at the scene of devastation as more rockets fired down at the vessels still standing on the Base's landing strip. Only one managed to get away and narrowly missed being struck as it gained height and soon shot up into the atmosphere. *She made it*, Mariam thought, recognising the vessel as that one that had brought death to her home.

"Quick there may be some survivors," Mariam said as she quickly got back into her car. The others followed suit, but General Faisal was less than optimistic about the prospect of finding anyone alive in the burning rubble.

"We have to head for the caves, it's not safe here," Faisal protested.

"We can't leave them to die." Mariam insisted.

"They're already dead, we can't help them."

"Mariam. We need to go," Aisha added.

"Let me check for my son at least. I told him to stay behind. I have to see if he's okay." The Alsuwayreans couldn't argue with that and so they made their way into the base and stopped a few hundred metres from the burning rubble. As they approached on foot they could see the broken shuttles, their metal ripped opened and caved in, all of them charred and burning. The building was a heap of stone, flames leapt up between fallen stone pillars and crumpled staircases, as ash billowed in the air like grey snowflakes and slowly began to settle on the ground, the devastation around them, and across their faces. They called out to any survivors and listened for sounds of life, but there were none. They clambered over broken floors, walls, and the debris of the offices, and called again and again. As they were about to turn back, Faisal heard it first. A rhythmic tapping of stone on metal, they all heard it then and quickly searched for the source. Grabbing a heavy stone block together form either end, Mariam and Faisal succeeded in shifting it enough for it to slide down a slope of stone and debris and beneath found a small hollow under a steel beam in which Colonel Khan was lying, covered in dust. His legs were clearly broken and bleeding and lying at twisted, unnatural angles to his body. He clutched a small stone in his right hand and was beating it repeatedly on the metal beam that had saved him from a swifter death. As they tried to lift him, he cried out in agony, every movement a knife through his twisted mangled legs, so they rested him back where he lay. "Did you see my son, Ibrahim?" Mariam demanded.

"Pain...Pain...Give me something...for the pain," He said as he sobbed, tears rolling down his cheeks and blood dripping from his mouth and nose and over his long moustache. But they had nothing to offer him. Faisal loosened his belt and tied it as a tourniquet high around the leg that was bleeding most and pulled it tight, causing the Colonel to scream into the night once more. Mariam called for an ambulance but as she brought the phone to her ear, a small shower of yellow lights descended like falling stars from above them and swept out over her city. Great booming thunder rolled towards them as yellow mushrooms of fire and dust bloomed up into the sky to their west. The lights flying back up into the heavens, leaving devastation in their wake. Again and again, they came, like angels falling from the sky to bring death, pounding her city relentlessly with each wave. She turned away, tears welling in her eyes, and she began clawing through the rubble, cracking, and splintering her fingernails as he threw rocks and stones down the slope of the pile on which she knelt. *He must be here. He might be alive somewhere. I have to help him.* "Ibrahim...Ibrahim," she called again and again.

Aisha gripped her shoulder as Colonel Khan's wailing became weaker. "There is nothing further to do. He may have gone with Dr Schaffer, we don't know. We have to help the others. Will you come with me?"

"I can't leave him. He is all I have left in the world," Aisha took her in an embrace then and held her as Mariam sobbed into the shoulder of her silk shawl. Khan had become silent as he finally succumbed to his wounds and Faisal stood up, balancing precariously on the rocks beneath him.

Together they made their way down and back to their car. Faisal drove as Aisha guided Mariam into the back of the car. They headed towards the Kirishima caves with Mariam indicating directions as she sobbed. *I failed him, I failed them all*, she thought.

Chapter 17

Master Nobuhide flew his shuttle with the same grace he used when fighting. Not easily bestirred to anxiety, he weighed options quickly and carefully and then made decisions and kept to them, rarely changing his mind unless new salient information emerged, or the situation demanded it. He had long ago accepted the inevitably of death and as such it held little fear for him. He hoped his decisions would prove sound, but all he could do was trust that he had made the best decisions with the information he had, and let the fates fall where they would. He was being pursued by two Imperial fighters now and he calmly dodged and weaved to avoid the plasma bolts they fired, sometimes rolling the craft to avoid being hit sometimes pulling up, and sometimes diving, in an effort to prevent his movements from becoming predictable to his droid pursuers. His younger brother Nobunaga sat beside him in the craft but was less serene. He clutched at the arms of his seat and yelled in fear every time a plasma bolt flew over their small shuttle, sometimes jarring the vessel as it clipped a wing or scarred their fuselage. Nobunaga was handling the makeshift plasma cannon that Dr Schaffer's team had fitted to the roof of the vessel but had so far only managed to destroy two of the many enemy fighters assembled to destroy them.

The small fleet of Carthagian shuttles had been overwhelmed by the hundreds of fighters that hovered in rows in high orbit around Carthage almost midway between the planet and its moon. Below them the city was being decimated by bombing runs made by the fighters whilst reports from Cyrus indicated a small invasion force of five fighters had landed north of the city close to the Duke's mine, though it was not clear why they had done so. Anyone who got out of the city in time would be heading for sanctuary in the Kirishima caves but most, he knew, either had not made it there or would not survive the journey. Hundreds of thousands of people below would be dead or dying.

Three of the Carthagian fleet had been destroyed…so far. Nobuhide glanced at the clock on the dashboard before him. *Only three minutes until the Alsuwayreans arrive,* he thought. He didn't know the exact time of their arrival, but General Faisal had indicated an approximate time and that was enough to pin all their hopes. We just need to hold out for a little longer, he said as he flew over an Imperial shuttle and ordered Nobunaga to fire.

The Imperial vessel exploded in flame. "Three!" he counted.

Cyrus' voice suddenly boomed through their open communication channels. "Master Nobuhide, I have detected a spacetime distortion closing in forty-five degrees to your starboard side and at an inclination of seventy degrees and at a distance of two thousand kilometres. I believe the Alsuwayreans are arriving."

"Thank you, Cyrus," Nobuhide said with relief. "This tail is irritating me. I'm going to spin the craft around to cut it off Make sure you fire on these assholes as soon as I turn," he instructed his brother. With Nobunaga ready on the controls, Nobuhide suddenly reversed his engines and fired his aft and rear side thrusters and spun the vessel around. The shuttle creaked under the strain and Nobunaga let loose several volleys of flaming plasma as the vessel turned suddenly. Their plasma bolts found their mark and both Imperial fighters exploded momentarily into balls of yellow and red flame. "Five!" Nobuhide shouted.

He turned the shuttle to the bearing Cyrus had indicated and waited for the reinforcements to arrive, but as he did so, he noticed the Imperial vessels were also turning in the same direction from where a blue hue of a spacetime distortion was beginning to appear. "Oh no," he muttered as the first of the Alsuwayrean fighters suddenly appeared out of the blue haze. Then another and another, all suddenly appearing as if from nowhere. But as soon as they appeared they were picked off by the Imperial fighters and destroyed. Some appeared suddenly, only to crash headlong into the debris cloud of the fighters that had been destroyed before them and were destroyed themselves. "Oh no," Nobuhide said again. He turned his vessel around and headed for a region of space just behind the rows of Imperial fighters and contacted Cyrus. "Cyrus, the Alsuwayreans are being slaughtered. We can't do much more. I need you to initiate the singularity plan we discussed. Send signals to the other Carthagian fighters to hand over control to you and assemble them on my position in perpendicular planes to me. Got it."

"Master Nobuhide. Dr Schaffer and Duchess Mariam were opposed to this plan."

"I know. The Duchess only wanted to use it as a last resort. Well, this is the time for last resorts. The colony is destroyed. Everything is lost. This is the last Hail Mary we have. Do it now please. That's an order. And take control of this shuttle also."

"Yes sir. Understood. I will contact the other shuttles."

"How will we get out?" Nobunaga asked.

"Get into your suit. We're going to head across to one of the shuttles with the others."

Within a minute, six other Carthagian shuttles arrived in their proximity. Five quickly assembling in perpendicular planes relative to Nobuhide's shuttle, which was also moved by Cyrus into its designated position. Only one of the shuttles remained, out of the formation.

Hatches began to open on all of the shuttles in the formation and men began floating out into space dressed in their emergency space suits. As they did so the remaining shuttle flew in close and collected the men. Inside, the seventh shuttle the cockpit was crowded as fourteen men in their emergency spacesuits huddled together to look out of the shuttle's front window. Once aboard himself, Nobuhide looked out at the formation and gave instruction to the shuttle's pilot and spoke through the shuttle's communicator to Cyrus. "Okay, let's pull back to a safe distance. Cyrus, begin firing the Alcubierre engines on my mark."

The shuttle drew back to a distance of one hundred kilometres and once Nobuhide had given the go ahead, the men aboard could see a vague blue haze forming quickly in the centre of the six-shuttle formation. All the while, Imperial fighters continued destroying Alsuwayrean fighters as soon as they made their appearance in Carthagian space. The blue cloud within the formation soon resolved into a blue sphere and slowly but surely began to expand. The shuttles wavered slightly in their positions their thrusters and jets firing to stabilise their own positions to maintain formation. The blue sphere began to expand faster and faster until suddenly the blue hue of the sphere disappeared as the sphere expanded suddenly to consume all six of the shuttles which generated it.

It's working, Nobuhide knew. They could see the light of the planet below and the sun in the distance refracted across the sphere's surface and the light of stars behind the black hole suddenly began to form a bright halo of golden light around it as its blue hue dissipated. The sphere appeared to spin and as it did a bright gold accretion disc began to form, just as Dr Schaffer had predicted.

The debris of nearby shuttles and the Imperial fighters themselves began to pull towards the black hole, debris falling into it and lost to sight as they passed the accretion disc of the hole. The last Carthagian shuttle in which Nobuhide and his men were crowded, then began to creak and slide towards the hole. "We have to go. Now," Nobuhide instructed, as the pilot fired up the shuttle's jets and began to fly down to the planet. It took a few seconds longer than it would have normally done, to pull away, but eventually they freed themselves of the pull on their ship and made their way down towards the Kirishima caves. Imperial fighters closest to the hole now began to disappear into it. Alsuwayrean fighters were still arriving, but the line of Imperial fighters were now fighting with their jets to stay out of the gravitational pull of the black hole at their backs and more and more of the Alsuwayrean fighters were making their way across towards the planet surface unharmed. The ominous black sphere of involuted spacetime, was growing larger and larger marked only by its halo and the accretion disc that circled it, drawing in more and more of the Imperial fighters, that floated at its lip and any stray Alsuwayrean fighters that wandered too close. It was an incarnation of pure doom, a silent growing malevolence in the void of space. But it was also hope.

Chapter 18

Aboard the Imperial Shuttle heading to Hydrax Prime, Ibrahim and Dr Schaffer stretched back in the two pilot seats and relaxed. There was nothing more to be done. Dr Schaffer had setup the droid to be deaf and blind and ready to be powered on to deliver her virus.

"How will we let the fleet know that the hack is done?"

"I would expect it should become clear from the behaviour of the fleet; they should be drifting around helplessly so anyone left in our fleet and the Alsuwayreans should be able to pick them off easily."

"Let's hope they do. Is there anything you think we need to go over in preparation?"

"No, I think we're good. I've double checked everything and we're good to go. I just need to power up the droid and as soon as it's authenticated and the sync begins, I'll let the virus loose. It won't take long. Then we high tail it out of there before the droids come back online and we're blown away by their fighters. I've also disabled the droid's motor functions, eyes, and ears, so it won't be able to talk to us or see what we're doing either."

"Sounds good."

Colonel Khan and his men had provisioned the craft with ration packs in anticipation it would be used in battle and both Dr Schaffer and Ibrahim settled back in their seats to eat.

"I could really do with a cigarette right about now." Schaffer said as she chewed on a protein energy bar.

Before long they decided to get some rest and, setting an alarm to wake them before they arrived, they laid back and closed their eyes. Dr Schaffer was sound asleep and snoring loudly within minutes, whereas Ibrahim remained awake thinking about all that could go wrong with their plan and how to counter each of the possible setbacks. Eventually, the gentle hum of the Alcubierre engines took him, and he drifted off into sleep and the memory of his encounter with the Mahdi returned vividly to him.

"The infidels invaded our lands, stole our wealth, and murdered our people. And where were our great leaders when this was happening? They were getting drunk, gambling, and whoring with their infidel friends, spending the wealth that Allah had gifted them, on lavish trinkets, boats, and jewels, while their brothers and sisters were starving and dying at the hands of their infidel friends." Ibrahim couldn't deny there was truth in those words. *"If I were leading them, I would have done better,"* he told the Mahdi in his dream. *"A leader should serve his people, not be served."* He then saw in his dream a tall golden man with a knife in hand, towering over hundreds of people dressed in rags, who prostrated before him in prayer. He saw the man lift his father by his neck and stab him through his chest and then fling his lifeless body across a wall. *"Why did you do it?"* He questioned the golden man.

"You do not understand, you can never grapple with my superior wisdom. For I am a god, and you are but a grain of

sand in the desert, a fly in the wake of my passing," the golden man replied to him as he threw the knife at Ibrahim and stabbed him through the chest.

Ibrahim awoke with a start and felt his chest where the dream knife had struck him and remembered where he was, the planned hack, and Dr Schaffer. She continued to snore beside him loudly with a smile across her broad wrinkled face. *At least she's happy*, he thought. He tried to sleep again but this time sleep would not come. As he closed his eyes, he could see the broken bodies of the dead all around him, the people killed by the Alsuwayreans in the Mahdi's cave, the people killed by the Mahdi's men in the mosque, and the butcher's boy, Salah, most of all. *"I wish I could have helped you,"* he said in his mind, to the boy.

Finally, their countdown alarm bleeped loudly, and Dr Schaffer sat up, rubbing the sleep from her eyes, and putting on her glasses. They were ten minutes from their destination. Ibrahim took a deep breath and made a small prayer with his hands cupped together, whilst Dr Schaffer made final checks of the droid and powered up her computers to make ready.

As the pale blue hue of the Alcubierre engines dissipated, they could see Hydrax Prime looming ahead of them; a giant ball of blue and white in the vast infinite blackness of space, its enormous red sun many millions of miles away in the distance. Without hesitation, Dr Schaffer powered up the droid and waited, watching her computer screen. After a brief moment, pages and pages of code began scrolling down her screen one line at a time as the droid was authenticated by the Alexion AI. "We're in," Dr Schaffer exclaimed as the code stopped scrolling. She clicked a few keys on her keyboard. "I'm going to load it now." As her fingers danced on her keyboard, she suddenly paused. "What's this?" she said. "There are lots of files downloading. I'm not sure what this is."

"Just get the virus in, we don't have much time."

"Sure. Give me a second. I just need to get this to load. It's synchronising, but I got it," she said as she resumed her clicking on the keyboard.

As she was typing, the proximity alarms on the shuttle's dashboard began to bleep and Ibrahim looked up to see a Carthagian shuttle being chased by two Imperial fighters, a few hundred kilometres away. He swung the vessel towards them and powered up the plasma cannons.

"What are you doing?" Dr Schaffer asked.

"Helping," he replied.

He shot a volley of plasma blasts at one of the Imperial fighters which took a direct hit and exploded into a momentary blame of yellow and red flame, as large fragments of the vessel, flew apart. The other fighter fired on the Carthagian vessel and clipped its rear, sending it spinning. Ibrahim shot again and destroyed the remaining Imperial fighter. He then flew close to the Carthagian vessel, staying approximately fifty feet away, as it span down in an uncontrolled spiral towards the planet. He radioed. "Carthagian vessel, this is Ibrahim Hazahari of Carthage, what is your status? Who are you?"

"Please don't shoot. The shuttle's jets are disabled. I can't stabilise it."

"Who are you?"

"Zaid Abbas. Chief Medical Officer. Look, I'm caught in the planet's gravity. I need to come aboard your craft."

"What shall we do?" Ibrahim asked Dr Schaffer. "I'm tempted to blow his ass up or let him burn up in the atmosphere. What do you think?"

"The virus is in. Let's get him and head back. We're not murderers."

Ibrahim thought on that for a moment, then radioed back to the doctor. "Okay, put on your emergency spacesuit and use the emergency hatch in the ceiling to get free of the craft we'll pick you up."

"Okay, I'll try," the doctor replied.

After a few minutes, Ibrahim saw the hatch on the ceiling of the craft swing open violently as the air in its cabin, and scraps of paper and ration packs were sucked out into the void of space. Dr Abbas then climbed up and out, wearing his bright blue emergency spacesuit. He clambered on top of the craft, his movements slow and awkward as he gripped the shuttle's spinning outer hull and then pushed himself free. He was spinning as he floated away from the craft and Ibrahim could see the doctor carried a black leather bag slung across his back. He gently nudged his vessel closer using the shuttle's thrusters and aligned himself in the path of the traitor. Then both he and Dr Schaffer donned their emergency suits and checked their droid passenger was securely strapped into the chair in which she had been placed. Once ready he opened the fuselage ramp as a sudden burst of air escaped from the shuttle. Once Dr Abbas was inside, Ibrahim closed the shuttle ramp and began repressurising the craft.

Once that task was complete, he took off his helmet and drew his plasma handgun pointing it at the doctor.

"What are you doing? I'm one of you. I'm a Carthagian," the doctor sounded surprised as he also pulled off his helmet and let it float in the air around him.

"I know who you are and what you are…traitor."

"Traitor? What? I'm not a traitor. I was trying to end this war. You don't understand. I know what they were after, why they were attacking us. I have it here."

"What are talking about?"

"Look…here," Abbas said as he opened the bag he was carrying and drew out the glass box with the apple and the stone tablet. He pushed the tablet across to Dr Schaffer and tossed the glass box to Ibrahim. Both items floated in the weightlessness of the shuttle to their recipients and both Ibrahim and Dr Schaffer looked at one another, bemused. The tablet was inscribed with a series of vertical and angular lines in three distinct columns but meant nothing to Dr Schaffer. Ibrahim meanwhile turned the glass box over in his hand and inspected the apple within with the bite taken from it. "What the hell is this?"

"The Emperor is after it. That's all I know. That's why he has been drilling all over the colonies. It's not for lithium like we thought, it was for this."

"It's just an apple," Ibrahim looked at Schaffer and lowered his gun.

"Look. I don't know why, but the Emperor believes this is an alien apple of some kind. I presume it is more significant than it looks."

"Let me see. We downloaded a lot of files when we did the hack. Let me check if anything is mentioned here," Dr Schaffer said turning back to her computer.

"Hack. What hack? And why did you call me a traitor?" Abbas asked.

"Sit your ass in that chair and shut the fuck up. You hacked Cyrus, almost brought him down, didn't you? You bastard. Why did you do it?" Ibrahim had pulled the gun again and used it to indicate a chair behind the pilot's seats, next to the naked droid.

"We need to get out of here!" Dr Schaffer said, tugging on Ibrahim's arm and pointing out of the front window. He turned to look and saw at least ten Imperial fighters heading straight for them. He sat in his seat and selected the navigation data for Carthage and began powering up the Alcubierre engines. The fighters were closing in and Ibrahim could see an orange glow developing in their plasma cannons, just as the blue haze of the Alcubierre engine enveloped their ship and swept them way from danger.

"That was close," Dr Schaffer said as she returned to scrolling through the files she had downloaded from the Emperor's AI.

Ibrahim turned to Zaid and pulled up the handgun to point at him, wagging it towards the seat, he wanted the captive to take. Zaid ignored the instruction and seemed completely indifferent to the gun. "You're Ibrahim, aren't you? I've met you before a long time ago when you were a child. You probably don't remember me, do you?"

"So what?"

"It's a shame I never got to know you. I would have liked that, I think…Have you ever wondered why you don't look anything like your father?"

"I look more like my mum, so what's it to you?"

"No, actually you *do* look like your father, but just not the man you've been told was your father."

"What are you trying to say?"

"I'm saying Ichiro Hazahari was not your father. Your mother has been lying to you your entire life."

"Shut the fuck up!" he spat the words at the traitor but felt a deep apprehension at what he might say next, but deep down he already knew what the man would say next.

"I am your father. Look at yourself. You have my nose, my eyebrows, my mouth. The only thing you don't have is my eyes."

Ibrahim looked at the man's face. Studied it, the nose, the eyes, the mouth. He saw the resemblance, saw it the moment he came inside the shuttle, but he didn't want to confront the possibility that his mother had been lying to him, that she could have conceived him with this vile man. That was just too much, too incomprehensible. His head began to swim as the implications of the revelation began to unfold in his mind, unbidden, as he struggled to push the thoughts away.

"Ichiro was my father. You have no proof," he said boldly, trying to sound confident.

"Sure. Your mother has a birthmark on her left thigh. I've seen it, a small pale brown patch, quite high up on the inside. How would I know that if I hadn't seen her naked?"

His mother did indeed have such a birthmark, Ibrahim knew. He had seen it when they went swimming on one of the colonies they had visited for a holiday. *Maybe he saw her swimming too*, he thought, but he knew his mother was always careful not be so exposed in the company of men. He could see in the way he spoke that Zaid believed what he was saying and as he watched the man. He knew everything he was saying was true. As he made this realisation, his world began to crumble. His father's family that he thought of as his own, their trips to his father's house in Kyoto, the stories his father had told him about the people he thought were his ancestors, the watch his father had given to him as a teenager which Ichiro told him was a family heirloom. *But, of course, he wasn't family at all, just some man who lived with his mother and told him always to be honest and truthful but lied and lied.* His sense of himself and his place in the world, all of it was crumbling, all of it lies. He suddenly felt lost in a way he had never experienced before, unable to separate the truth from the lies about who he was. But mostly, he felt betrayed and angry. *My mother did this to me. She's to blame. She lied to me. She's been lying to me every day of my life. How can I ever trust her? What else is she lying about?* "Ichiro was my father," he said again, but the words rang hollow without conviction and both he and Zaid knew then, that Ibrahim accepted the falseness of that statement.

"Your mother and I were in love. We were happy and the man you call your father stole her from me. We were meant to be together, but she ran away with him. She lied to me, and she lied to you."

"Stop it, stop talking!" Zaid's words were pecking at his mind, irritating, agitating him, angering him.

"I won't. You know it's true I can see that. You've known it your whole life, haven't you?"

"Just stop…stop!" *why won't he just shut up,* he thought as the pecking words became hammering nails.

"Your mother lies, she lies, and she lies and every night she ran back to her Japanese boyfriend and lied to him, told him you were his, even when she was fucking me."

"Just shut up!" Ibrahim raised the gun again now, pointing it at Zaid, who continued to ignore it, as if it were just some plastic toy that was no threat to him.

"She was a sweet lay, I have to admit. She would let me do things that even I could not believe. Your mother is quite the whore, you know, when she wants to be. And boy, did she want to be with me!"

That was enough for Ibrahim. He squeezed the trigger and let loose a ribbon of orange plasma that struck Zaid in his smug, smiling face. His head erupted in flame that engulfed his whole head as the flame became a fireball within the weightless cabin. His eyeballs exploded as the plasma struck him and his smile turned into a scream. He screamed, and screamed, a terrible shrieking that reminded Ibrahim, for a moment, of the mosque attack on Carthage. The on-board fire alarms immediately began to blare, and halon gas sprayed down from the ceiling to extinguish the flames. The gas began to fill the cabin in a thick mist and Dr Schaffer quickly flushed the cabin with new oxygen which, for a moment, reignited the traitor's flaming head as his lifeless body floated backwards in the cockpit and bumped into the door at the rear. The smell of burnt flesh filled the cabin.

"You okay?" Dr Schaffer asked, looking with concern at her friend.

"No. Not really. But I feel a lot better now that that bastard's dead."

"Okay. Just take it easy. Maybe give me the gun. You're a bit emotional right now, it's best not to have any weapons in your hands when you're emotional. It's a general rule of thumb that I found works well for me."

Ibrahim floated the weapon over to the scientist and moved himself into the pilot's seat, strapping himself down so he did not float out of it. Dr Schaffer took the weapon and tucked it into her waistband below the overhang of her belly. She then removed Zaid's body with its charred head, half hanging off at the neck, and strapped it down into one of the seats in the rear cabin and returned.

Ibrahim was silent, looking blankly at the blinking lights and buttons of the dashboard, his ungloved hands clenched in tight fists. "He was a traitor who sold us all out, he deserved to die, but you can't trust anything he said. When we get back, you ask your mother about it. Maybe it's true, maybe it's not, but you owe your mother the opportunity to tell you the truth herself, rather than assume something about her that isn't true. Don't you think?" Ibrahim looked up at her and she could see tears welling in the corners of his eyes.

"I don't know who I am anymore. They were all lying to me. Everyone. Why should I forgive that? I haven't done anything wrong. They have. They're the ones that should be punished for it. Not me."

"No one's punishing you for anything. Let your mother explain."

"Sure doesn't feel that way. Was she fucking him? Did she plan all this to get rid of my father? Who knows, maybe she sent me to Alsuwayra to die, so she could be with him, her lover."

"I'm sure your mother loves you and if it is true and she didn't tell you, I am sure she had her reasons. But I think it's much more likely this is just another lie from a man who almost killed us all with his little trick on Cyrus. Now listen, let's park that idea and come have a look at this. The droid synchronised with the AI when we linked-up and there are a lot of files to look through." She pulled up the holographic images of text on her computer and began going through them so Ibrahim could see as well. "It's downloaded the central core files of the Emperor's AI. We could actually power her up here if we wanted to."

"Let's not. I really don't need that thing coming back to life," he replied to her distractedly.

Finally, she came across a file that mentioned an apple. "Hey, look here, check this out." indicating to the holographic display of text. "It says the Emperor has been looking for a 'key' placed somewhere amongst the new colonies which he believes is alien in origin and belongs to a race of humanoids called the 'Eroehznayn'. I think that's how you say it. Apparently, these aliens are superior compared to us somehow and left this key as a way of communicating with them."

"And that's this apple? How?" Ibrahim looked at the glass box with the apple inside, wondering if it were true, that some alien race could truly be out there and had left this to be found by humans.

"Apples are for eating and this one's already had a bite taken out of it. Maybe the tablet gives instructions, but I imagine it just says something like: *Eat me*."

"So if one of us eats it, then what? We magically get transported to their planet, or something?" Dr Schaffer could see Ibrahim was emerging from his grief now.

"I have no idea, but there *is* one way to find out."

"Go for it," he said, handing her the box.

"Not me. You can count me out. I'm definitely *not* going to eat some alien apple. God knows what might happen."

"It's a shame I killed Abbas, or we could have fed it to him to see what happens".

"Yeah, but if it did work, would you have really wanted *him* to be the first human that these aliens meet? He wasn't exactly someone I would call a good representative of our species."

"Good point. I guess I'll have to do it then."

"You don't *have* to do anything. Why not wait until we get back and then discuss it with your mother."

"My mother…yeah. The one who's been lying to me my whole life."

"Okay maybe not her, but we could at least test it and make sure it's safe before you start chowing down on it."

"Look, we don't know if this hack has worked or not. Or what state the war is in and whether anyone is even still alive back there. I say take a bite and see if there are any aliens that suddenly transport us to their planet. I seriously doubt it. But *if* it's true, maybe we could get some help or an alien weapon or something that we can use on the Emperor. If there are such things as aliens that like to communicate using fruit! And if it's nothing, then we can share the apple, but we won't know unless we take a bite."

"I'm seriously not eating that. Someone's already taken a bite. *Hygiene* people! 'But look, it's up to you."

"Ok, I'm doing it. Let me just get this open." Ibrahim used his dagger to pry the box open and the top surface of the cube popped open easily with only a little pressure. He drew out the apple and sniffed it, turning it over in his hands. The surface of the apple was reddish gold and seemed to shimmer and sparkle in the light of the shuttle, but the only smell was of apple juice. "Here goes nothing," he said as he took a small bite next to where the apple had already been bitten. He chewed the chunk slowly and then swallowed, but nothing happened.

"So…what does it taste of?"

"Apple," he replied. "It's just an apple. Not a bad one too. Sweet. Sure you don't want some?"

Dr Schaffer shook her head watching him closely, but nothing appeared to be amiss. "How do you feel?"

"Hungry," he said. "It's just an apple, I'm telling you. It's nonsense, definitely not an alien artefact."

"Okay. Let's head home. Maybe don't eat the rest and we can get it tested when we get back, just to be sure."

"Okay sure," He returned the remainder of the apple to its box and pressed down the lid, sealing it again back in its environment. He was storing the apple in a cabinet to his side when he suddenly felt faint, his head began to spin, and he saw bright stars of red, yellow, gold, and blue, flooding down towards him, one after another in quick succession, as if he were falling headlong into a bottomless well filled with stars. He gripped the armrests of the pilot's seat, blanching his fingertips. "Oh…I don't feel well," he muttered.

"Hey. You okay?" Dr Schaffer asked as she quickly moved from her chair to his side, feeling for a pulse, which thankfully she found easily. He slipped into unconsciousness then, his breathing rapid and his pulse racing. She considered putting her fingers down his throat to force him to vomit but didn't want to take the risk of him choking or inhaling the vomitus. So instead she checked he was secure in his seat and reclined it as far as it would go. Then she turned to the dashboard and checked they're time to Carthage. *Oh, why did I let him eat it? That was so stupid…I have to get him back to*

Carthage...Now. She scoured the cockpit for a first aid kit but finding none she returned to his side. His face looked serene as if he just fallen into a deep sleep but beneath his eyelids, his eyes flickered and moved relentlessly.

Chapter 19

Stars flew past Ibrahim, swirling, churning, flame rippling in shades of yellow, white, and red; flew over him, beneath him, to either side, and through him and seared his eyes with the brightness of the light they cast. Each so magnificent, he could neither fathom their enormity, nor their shape. No heat or flame scorched him, and no sounds reached him expect the thumping of his heart and the quiet rasping of his quickened breath. He flew through the arms of enormous spiral galaxies that unfolded and refolded before him, some spinning and twisting as he swept over them, between them, and through them. He had never before known the vast beauty that enveloped him.

He struggled and twisted, tried to awaken, to overcome the hallucinogen he must surely have consumed in the apple bite he had taken, but it was of no use. He tried closing his eyes and turning away, but his eyes were already closed and still the vision flooded over him, through him, and around him. He tried to call out, to scream, to move his arms, and protest, but it was as if his body was paralysed, as if his mind had somehow been separated from its mastery of his physical form.

He saw a large blue planet looming ominously ahead that reminded him of Earth and, in that moment, knew he would surely be smashed to pieces on its land or drowned beneath the blue waves of its oceans as he rushed headlong towards its surface, unable to control his descent towards it, or its upward flight towards him. Down he flew, through clouds and past birds to fall into its ocean, passing shoals of fish and ancient whales, with enormous eyes, that seemed not to see him pass. Further he flew, down, down as the light around him faded, and into deep underwater trenches where the light did not penetrate. Further down into the oily black of its deepest depths he flew, down, consumed by the eye of a fish that rose up suddenly huge in his path. He flew into that black bottomless well and saw before him a shining silvery surface and through it he passed, as if flying through a soft, shimmering mirror. Down he flew, the nerves of the eye, extending before him like vast white highways stretching out into a dark oblivion, and then down between the cells of a nerve and into the cells themselves. Through dark curtains he passed and saw strange transparent structures floating past him and towering ovals as tall as skyscrapers, holding together bright distorted shapes that locked together and were then released to form a lengthening chain. Past a further dark curtain he flew, between its long strands and over a vast uncoiling helix. He saw vaguely hexagonal yellow and white structures arranged within the infinite spiral that extended far into the distance where the coiling helix looped and folded back over itself. Into those hexagonal structures he passed and saw a haze of vast globes locked closely together, each seemed to contain an entire universe. Down into one of those universes he flew, down between the clouds of planets and stars within them and then suddenly he was flying upwards. Passing out through the eye of the fish up from the deep trench, up from the planet's surface and across space and time. Through another a galaxy he passed, white and green aurora shimmering and flickering across the surface of a great, fiery, red star, its swirling, churning surface, a hell of infinite flame and heat. Across entire galaxies he passed, galaxies beyond count, over distances beyond comprehension, and finally...he arrived.

He was overwhelmed by the majesty of what he had experienced, the boundless beauty of the universe from the subatomic to the supra-galactic. He realised he had seen protons and electrons within atoms, and the vastness of galaxies billions of miles wide, and passed over incomprehensible distances of the void between them. He became filled with an incomprehensible sadness yet at the edge of it a profound gratitude, for the privilege of his vision, emotions that swirled and swelled within him to consume him. If he could open his eyes, he knew he would surely have been crying at the beauty of creation he had witnessed.

Stillness and darkness surrounded him then as if was back in the Alsuwayrean caves, groping in the utter and complete darkness, wishing for a light that would not come, for Jamal and Nobunaga to return with their torch, from wherever they were. Then he felt it. A presence, not malevolent, but welcoming. Silently probing his mind. He could feel her, a woman. The soft tendrils of her thoughts touching him like the tips of her fingers, as she whispered to him softly in a language he did not understand, a comfort in the dark. She asked him a question he knew, but he didn't understand. He tried to tell her, to speak his answer to her, and suddenly his mind was ablaze, a hundred fires sweeping over his brain and through the backs of his eyes. A searing pain that lasted for a few seconds, before ebbing away.

"Welcome," the woman said softly. Ibrahim could hear a shimmering sound, like tiny bells tinkling softly as she spoke, but he could understand her. He could feel her presence in the darkness around him and he felt at ease, relaxed, and safe.

"Hello? I can't see you. Who are you?"

"You will see me in time. But first, I must prepare you. You are safe, trust in me and my voice and you will not fear. Welcome, Ibrahim of Carthage."

"You know me? How do you know who I am?"

"I will answer your questions in time. I have felt your mind and your soul, I know much of you, but not all. Your minds are more complicated to navigate than ours, more layers of lies and secrets. Secrets within secrets and lies within lies. It is of your nature, not of your doing."

"Who are you? What are you? Where am I?" In his mind, he was shouting at the woman, suddenly annoyed at his dislocated, disoriented feeling, the blindness of his vision, and the lack of explanation.

"Calm yourself, and I will explain." As she said the words, he felt suddenly calmer and more relaxed as if her words alone had command over his body, a body he could not feel in the dark around him.

"Your mind is with me, but your body remains where it was. The fruit you consumed separates the mind from the body and brings your mind upon the ether that connects us, across the universe to us so that we might communicate. When you are ready, we will return your mind to your body. You are safe."

"Who are you?"

"My name is Iru-la-nou-ris," she said her name slowly, taking care to sound out the syllables for Ibrahim. "*We* are Ero-ehz-nay-n. Our home is *Nora-minir* and it is very, very, far from your home. Yet we have watched your species for many of your millennia and studied your growth and your change. We have observed you in the creation of your wars, your kingdoms, your empires, your travels out into space, and your many, many, failures. We have at times gifted your people with knowledge, that you might avoid calamity and brought others to us, so that you may know us."

"You didn't stop the Great War on Earth," Ibrahim was trying to take it all in. But he could not yet bring himself to believe. *I must be dreaming*, he thought.

"We are not the custodians or guardians of your planet or your people. We have watched and we have guided at times, but the journey your species *must* take is its own *to* take, where it will. We have invited you to meet with us that you may know you are not alone in this garden and that other better forms exist," she replied.

"Better, how exactly?"

"I can feel that you do not believe my words, but this is not a deception. Perhaps hold your judgement for another time, for I only speak the truth to you now, and now is the only time you have to hear me."

"Okay," he replied grudgingly.

"When our Lord created you, He created many, worlds and raised you above *most* of the species that He populated in His universe…most…but not all.

"The Eroehznayn were created to be above *all* other species in the universe. Still, despite our gifts, some of our kind still err. Still, some do not heed their Lord and revolt against their purpose, but that is our burden and our challenge to bear. You have yours and we, ours."

"Okay…So what makes you so superior to everyone on my planet?"

"We have known your peoples for many millennia and watched you grow and change, waiting to see if you were worthy, to see if you were capable of overcoming the impediments that our Lord tested you with. You see, in His greater wisdom, He granted you a terrible nature. A nature in which the principal instinct of your species, is a greed only for your own selves. A boundless greed that can never be satiated. Using this greed, you have succeeded to advance far, to gain knowledge and become closer to your Lord, but your greed has now led you to a place from which there is no path forward, and so you must fall backwards until you can rise again.

"Our scholars have concluded that this impulse for greed for yourselves has resulted in your people being forever locked in competition with one another, rivalling one another to determine which of you can spend the brief time our Lord has granted you, to accumulate the greatest number of objects for yourselves. Objects that have cost you much in terms of the destruction that has been caused by them, or for them, but which of themselves benefit you not, and which you must always put aside when your time is at an end. Your greed is bound together with an immensity of fear, an instinctive inclination towards fear, and you have tortured and slaughtered so many of your own kind in numbers beyond count and destroyed the animals and plants that were created be of benefit to you, simply because of this fear.

"Your inclination is always to bend towards your insatiable greed and your immense fear. Therein must lie the test our Lord has bestowed upon you, but which you are unable to perceive, unable to comprehend and unable to overcome."

"We have done great things. Our scientists have created cures for diseases and made huge discoveries which have helped people out of poverty and enabled us to travel to the stars and establish colonies across the galaxy. Sure, there has been war and the Earth was damaged, but there has always been war and often it has been necessary in order to protect people who can't protect themselves, to defend the weak," Ibrahim protested.

"Your species have created poverty and war through the choices you as individuals have made again and again, and your wars were truly more in service of your greed, than in the defence of the weak, as you say. We have watched you collaborate, yes. Your people have undertaken great journeys, built some technologies, and solved many difficult problems. But always, beneath the surface, the true impulse driving even *these* achievements has been your own individual greed, your own need to accumulate more objects simply that you can convince yourselves of your own value. Such is the empty nature of your form and the civilisations you have built."

"Okay, so how are you different?"

"The nature of the Eroehznayn is a mercy to us. We have been gifted with the ability to feel the emotions of others, and this endows us with the ability to truly understand a thing from the perspective of another being. This comprehension of others is not limited to the emotions of our own species but extends to the emotions of the higher animals and even the higher plants around us, which we can feel and understand. It is no easy thing to slaughter an animal or destroy a tree when you can feel the fear and pain it suffers as its life is drawn from it.

"While we are also inclined towards greed, ours is not the greed of accumulating objects, nor the greed of power over others. Ours is a greed for knowledge, a hunger to understand the universe and all it holds within the dark mantle of its infinite embrace. For us it is not necessary to convince ourselves of our own value, it is a thing ordained that we understand intimately, instinctively. We learn, we teach, we lift up others when they fall, so that all might benefit from what one benefits, and from the knowledge we collectively reveal."

"Sounds great!" he said mockingly.

"It is no easy thing to comprehend, I understand. When the nature of your insatiable greed is so embedded within your very essence, it is of your nature, not of your doing, and so it is difficult for you to stand apart from it and consider another way. But therein lies the vast distance between us."

"It's not an easy thing to understand, you're right. But if that is the way we have been created, surely we should embrace it."

"And accumulate as many petty objects as possible in the short time you have and destroy anything and anyone that comes between you and your possession of these things?"

"No…that…what you describe is what I am fighting against right now. We have an Emperor who rules over all the colonies that our people fled to, when the Great War happened on Earth. The Emperor killed my father and is threatening to kill everyone on my planet, and I have to stop him. That's why

I ate the fruit. I wanted to see it any of your people could help me."

"We are aware of your Emperor, and we can foresee that your destiny is intricately bound to his. It is true that occasionally among us, there are some who, like your people, pursue ambition, power, and selfish greed and in doing so, turn away from the righteous teachings of our common creator. In these cases, where we cannot reason with them, we are sometimes forced to fight them, in order to protect the Eroehznayn, the animals, and plants, who will otherwise become the victims of these ignorant few. This is just and so it is right."

"So, you agree it is right to fight the Emperor. You must have weapons? Will you help me?"

The being calling herself Irulanouris, paused then for a moment, clearly considering what to do. "The only assistance I can offer you is advice. To arm yourself with awareness of your soul, your own desires, temptations, and ambitions, and not to succumb to your fear, as the Emperor has done. You are enough as you are, you have intrinsic value, and nothing more that you possess will add to that value, except knowledge and gratitude to your creator for the mercies he bestows upon you. Do this and the destiny that is unfolding now can be averted, elsewise the destiny you will choose is subjugation of your people to the Emperor."

"That's not much help, I'm afraid." For a moment he thought he might get some tangible assistance in his war, but he felt her advice was useless to him. "I need weapons, something I can kill his droids with, not lessons in meditation and self-reflection!"

She was silent then, but still present. He could feel her as he could feel his own heartbeat, though his heart was on the other side of the universe from his mind. Her silence continued and so he spoke:

"Okay, look, the Emperor seems to have been after the apple I ate that brought me to you. He seems to want it badly enough to kill people for it. Do you know why he would want it so badly? Has he met your people before? Is he the one that are it before?"

"The *apple*, as you call it, was placed where we knew your people would find it, but only when your people had developed to a certain level of knowledge and technology. I placed it there myself, many of your centuries ago and have been waiting for it to be found. One of your people did find it a few of your years ago and I communed with that man. It may be the same man who seeks it now to return to us and learn more from us, or perhaps he wishes to find his way to us. If he truly is as misguided as you say it is perhaps better that he does not find it."

"Okay. So, I should hide it somewhere?"

"It is better for you, that you destroy it."

"If I destroy it, how will I ever speak to you again?"

"In time your people will find the other gifts we have left for you and one day, when your society has developed enough, you will be able to meet with us in person. Until that day, you must try to overcome the challenges you face on your own as it is only through such challenges that your people can grow. To you my advice is to humble yourself before your creator and walk not the path of vengeance, pride and greed."

"I understand, I think. May I see this planet of yours, *Noraminir*, I think you called it."

"Yes, that's right. Certainly. You are now ready for me to let the veil fall from your eyes."

Gradually, the darkness that had immersed Ibrahim fell away, and his vision brightened. Before him stood a strange looking, very tall, woman with a long thin neck and large heart shaped head and enormous dark eyes. Her nose was slender and straight, and her lips were thin. Her head was completely bald and the skin over her face, head and exposed arms and legs shone with a golden radiance that seemed to shimmer as she moved. *Irulanouris*, he thought, remembering the name she had proffered.

In his mind, Ibrahim turned his head and looked all around him. He appeared to be in an open garden with tall trees and flowers all around him, under a purple sky slashed with red at the horizon. Low bushes of flowers and leaves grew to the height of his waist and small red, blue, and green birds chirped at him from amongst the plants. In the distance he could see great shimmering towers of glass and metal with walkways and highway between upon which vehicles travelled. He could also see pyramids and domed buildings lit up with shimmering gold and bluish-white light. Other Eroehznayn walked in the gardens, all clad like Irulanouris in clothes of simple tunics that covered them from neck to knee but in all different colours, some white, some pale blue and some pale green. All of them had skin that shone with the same golden radiance.

Looking around, Ibrahim felt a profound sense of peace and calm wash over and through him. He wanted to stay, he realised. He felt he was home. A better more peaceful home than he had ever known.

Irulanouris approached him then. "It is time for you to go now, my friend. Think upon what I have told you of our people and the nature of your species. Arm yourself as I have advised and use the knowledge, I have gifted you, so that you may return to us when you are able. By the will of the Lord we will meet again."

"Thank you," he said quietly as he felt stupid tears welling in his eyes and he was once again shrouded in utter darkness.

Chapter 20

Ibrahim slowly regained consciousness, a pounding pain in his head welcomed him back to the Imperial shuttle, he and Dr Schaffer had used to attack the Emperor's synthetic intelligence that controlled the Emperor's droid fleet.

As the pain slowly ebbed, he was overcome by a certainty, a conviction so absolute, that he knew he could never doubt it. He had been touched by the divine, chosen to play his role in the grand design, necessary for the salvation and betterment of his species. He didn't know how he would do it, but he was sure it was his purpose to do. He *must* create a better society, one free of the malevolence between the tribes and nations of mankind, that would rise above the petty greed and entitlement that had destroyed Earth and he would make his nation the only nation of mankind and one worthy of the Eroehznayn.

He looked around at Dr Schaffer who was peering at him with big eyes, magnified by her thick lenses. "Hey, welcome back. How are you feeling? I lost you for a while there." She was visibly relieved he was awake, and a broad smile beamed across her wide face.

"I'm fine. Just had a seriously vivid dream. How long was I asleep?" He was reluctant to share his unique experience with the scientist. He felt he needed time to reflect on it.

"About four hours. I tried to wake you, but you were out cold. So, did you meet any little green men?"

"Nothing happened...it's just an apple. I told you."

Dr Schaffer was unconvinced. *Perhaps it was a toxin in the apple, but he's hiding something,* she thought. "Okay. Maybe I *will* have a bite then," she said, reaching for the glass box to which he had returned it.

"NO!" he shouted at her and grabbed for the box but as he grabbed for it, he knocked it from the scientist's grasp, and it floated away towards the rear of the cockpit.

"Okay. What is going on? Tell me everything," she demanded.

"It's just...I don't know how to say this...but the apple...it worked. My mind was transported, and I spoke to an alien woman. She told me how they have been watching us for thousands of years and left that apple for us to find when we got out to the colonies. They are waiting for us to develop ourselves to a point when we are sophisticated enough to come and meet with them. At the moment, we're still too primitive for them, you see. I told her about the Emperor and the war, and she said he might have eaten the apple before and visited them before, which may be why he wants the apple back. And she said we have to keep it away from him or destroy it, because he's so dangerous."

"So, you're saying that aliens exist, and you've met one?"

"Essentially, yes. That's what I'm saying."

"You sure you didn't have a bad reaction to the apple and just had a hallucination or a dream, or something?"

"Look. I know it sounds crazy, but I spoke to her. It's real."

"Okay, let's get back and get the apple tested. Maybe we could see if there are any toxins or drugs in the apple that could explain your…experience."

"No. We can't take it back. The Emperor's forces are all over Carthage right now, we have to hide it somewhere. Now."

"How? Where?"

"Look. We'll take it and bury it someplace. We'll find somewhere, a moon or something, and bury it somewhere."

"Okay. Okay," Dr Schaffer looked at him quizzically. Whatever Ibrahim had experienced had changed his demeanour and he seemed less agitated and more certain of himself, though she was still sceptical that he had actually spoken with an alien. *A toxin in the apple is much more plausible*, she thought. "Look, we're alone in the middle of nowhere. Let's just get to Carthage. Once we're there we'll contact your mother, explain everything, understand the situation with the war, and then decide where to hide it, or what to do with it."

"No, it's too risky, if we're captured by the Emperor's forces, they'll take it from us and give it to him, and he will become even more powerful and may even try to kill them, after he's finished killing us. We can't let that happen. I won't let that happen. We need to hide it."

"Okay. I'm fairly confident our hack will have worked and the Alsuwayrean forces should be here by now and would have flown in and destroyed them all. Let's get there, and as soon as we know what's happening, we'll find somewhere to bury it."

"We need to find a moon. Somewhere remote, somewhere the Emperor won't find it."

"We will, I promise."

Dr Schaffer asked him to detail everything he had experienced in his vision. He was reluctant at first, but slowly recounted his experience, the words and details returning to him as he spoke. The hours passed and before long, their timer indicated they were only a few minutes from Carthage.

"Okay, let's get ready. I'll man the weapons, just in case. You fly the shuttle. We'll connect with Cyrus almost immediately, I'm sure, and then we can find out what's going on. Hopefully, your mum and everyone made it to the caves, and all is well. Then we can drop off Abbas back there and go hide this thing,"

"Let's not tell anyone about the apple, okay? Just in case the Emperor has spies or can still hack Cyrus."

"Okay, agreed."

Chapter 21

The blue hue of the Alcubierre distortion enveloping the Imperial shuttle dissipated as they arrived at their destination, but rather than decelerate to a stop, the ship continued to move slowly in the direction of travel. Dr Schaffer was about to remark on the oddness of that anomalous movement, when she saw before her the reason for it, and gasped at the terrifying scene before her.

Directly ahead, an enormous black hole almost half the size of the Alsuwayrean moon was quickly drawing in stray debris as Imperial and Alsuwayrean fighters fired their jets in a futile attempt to escape its gravitational pull. As they struggled to escape, they fell backwards across the bright accretion disc of the hole and disappeared. Their light, and their crew unable to escape from the depths of the hell, Nobuhide had created. "Oh no," Dr Schaffer muttered. "Oh no…no, no no…Nobuhide you fool!" She looked down at the great yellow planet below them and could see a thin tendril of its blue atmosphere coiling out towards the black hole and down into its unfathomable black mouth. "It's drawing off the atmosphere from the planet. This is bad…very bad."

"How can we close it?"

"We can't. It's too big. It's enormous."

"We have to try."

Before Dr Schaffer could answer Ibrahim, they felt and saw their vessel pulled closer towards the monstrous void that stood before them. An Imperial fighter suddenly appeared on their radar behind them, and their proximity alarm began to blare. The vessel may have been following them, but they had no time to consider the implications of that. Ibrahim quickly swung the shuttle around and fired its jets and thrusters to try to escape the pull of its intense gravity. Had it been a moon or a planet, they would surely have broken free, but the intensity of the pull on their ship was too much for their jets and they continued to slide towards it. "What shall I do?" Ibrahim asked.

"I don't know if there is anything we can do," Dr Schaffer replied defeated.

"Okay, I have an idea." Ibrahim thumped instructions into the shuttle's navigation computer and began firing up the Alcubierre engine once more.

"What are you doing?"

"Getting us out of here," he replied. "I've plotted a course back to Hydrax Prime. I'm hoping the Alcubierre distortion will pull us out."

"Okay that might work."

The blue hue of the Alcubierre engines began to form around the shuttle and as it grew, the shuttle's slide toward the hole began to slow.

"It's working!" Dr Schaffer exclaimed. But their escape was short lived. An Alsuwayrean fighter some distance away, and below them fired a bolt of plasma at them, clearly mistaking them for one of the Emperor's fleet. The bolt narrowly clipped their wing as it veered off towards the hole behind them. But the impact was enough to send the shuttle into a spin and Ibrahim fought with the jets and the thrusters as the blue hue of the spacetime distortion enveloped them. He stabilised the craft but nevertheless they slid helplessly into the black hole.

They knew they were in the grasp of the black hole, as soon as the ration packs and other objects floating in the cockpit immediately fell to its floor. They could hear the stress on the metal hull as the gravity intensified and the fabric of the thin metal holding the void of space at bay, creaked, and squealed around them. Both Ibrahim and Dr Schaffer quickly checked their space suits, making sure they were sealed tight. "It won't really matter. We're both dead now anyway," Dr Schaffer said.

The hue of the Alcubierre engine was all they could see before them and gave the cockpit a sickly blue glow. The vessel trembled and shook under the strain of intense gravity and both passengers could barely move their arms. They felt as if some massive weight was pressing down on them both. A few flakes of the gold paint from the shuttle's ceiling and dashboard, fluttered down to the floor of the vessel like confetti as the small metal vessel cried out in groans and creaks.

"A singularity within a singularity," Dr Schaffer muttered, barely audible to Ibrahim above the last gasps of the dying shuttle.

"What's that?"

"We've created a naked singularity and put it inside a naked singularity…It's just…I wonder."

"What?"

"Well, we might…" A loud roar cut her off as the blue haze before them suddenly resolved into a swirling, spinning, blue-walled tunnel with only blackness beyond. All around the haze of the distortion now formed the walls of the tunnel and they were racing forwards, propelled forwards, not under the force of their jets, but dragged or thrown by the forces of gravity and distorted spacetime. The shuttle's metal squealed at them as the force of gravity pushed down on its joints and seals. The speed of their travel pushed them both back into their seats; the muscles of their faces pushed backwards in hideous broad smiles that revealed their teeth, their eyes wide and staring at whatever lay ahead in the dark. Forward they flew, forever forward, until eventually they were still and the blue hue of the tunnel that had taken them there, dissipated as silently and as suddenly, as if it had never been there. But somehow, they were alive, and their vessel was intact.

"What was that?" Ibrahim said as he pulled off the round helmet of his suit and took a deep breath.

"I think we just became the first people to travel through an actual Einstein-Rosen bridge. A wormhole."

"A wormhole?"

"It's always been theoretical, but the idea was that if you could manipulate gravity and distort spacetime as we do with our A-cube engines. You could build a wormhole to traverse mind boggling distances of space in a few seconds. But no-one's ever attempted it before. Oh my! This is something." Dr Schaffer was smiling broadly.

"Okay let's see where we are, we still need to hide this apple and get back. Hopefully this time, without flying into Nobuhide's black hole."

"Sure." They both set about checking navigation charts and sensors. In front of their vessel, out of the front window, she could see a large yellow planet, which looked much like Carthage, but the fighters and debris that were floating in orbit all seemed to have disappeared, and so too had the enormous black hole. Dr Schaffer used the thrusters to pan the craft around and no sign of it was visible. *Could we have closed the hole?* she thought.

Ibrahim rose to fetch the apple still in its glass box and the stone tablet that accompanied it and placed them back in Zaid's bag. He then went to fetch some ration packs and a tube of water.

"Ibrahim. Can you come here for a second?" Dr Schaffer called to him from the cockpit.

Ibrahim returned to the pilot's seat. "What's up? Have you found where we are?"

"I haven't found where we are, but I did pick up a weak signal from the International Space Station…NASA's International Space Station."

Ibrahim looked out of the shuttle's front window down at the yellow planet before him. "The International space station. How can that be? There *is* no International Space station and no NASA."

"There hasn't been for many years, you're right. But I picked up a transmission. It's a conversation between a space shuttle and the station, discussing docking procedure."

"Maybe you picked up a recording. Or it's just the echo of a transmission that's only just reached here."

"No. It's not a recording, definitely not and I can calculate from the level of degradation of the message that it hasn't travelled that far. I estimate the message has been travelling for around about ten Earth-years, which would put *us* somewhere in the vicinity of the new colonies. Where exactly, I can't say because the computer's navigation is all scrambled since we passed through the wormhole."

"Hang on. I don't get it. The International Space Station was destroyed, what sixty years ago, so how is it possible that the transmission was created ten years ago."

"That's my point. I don't think we have travelled far in terms of distance from the black hole, but in terms of time, I think we have travelled into the past. Fifty or so Earth-years into the past."

Ibrahim could only laugh at that. "Come on, that can't be. How can we have travelled through time? That's mad!"

"Space, time, mass, energy, and gravity are all intrinsically linked together. I'm not an expert but somehow, we created a wormhole and passed through time. The timestamps on the message and the fact the message exists, are proof of that."

Ibrahim was silent for a while, brooding on that idea for a while. "No. It can't be. That's just crazy!"

"Look," she said as she played the crackly broken communication and showed him the timestamp embedded within the message as metadata. He sat looking at the timestamp, bewildered.

"Okay. Let's say you're right and we have travelled back fifty years. How do we get back?"

"That, I don't know."

"Can't we just create…no. Okay what *can* we do?"

"Okay look there." Dr Schaffer swung the craft around and pointed to a large red star in the distance. "I'm pretty sure that's the Hydraxian star that Hydrax Prime orbits. I think the only thing to do is head there and maybe work out what we do, if we can find other people there."

'Your destiny is intricately bound to his', he remembered. "Will there be anyone there? I mean if we've travelled into the past, won't the planet be uninhabited. Why don't we go back to Earth? Hey maybe we can stop the Great War before it begins."

"Honestly, if I could think of a way to stop that war, I would, but I have no idea what direction to travel in, for Earth. At least the Hydraxian star gives us a heading. And if I remember correctly, the Emperor first arrived on Hydrax Prime around fifty years ago with his AI, so maybe in this timeline he's not a bad guy and we can get his help. At the very least, we know there is a lot of water there and probably something to eat. These ration packs won't last very long. So we can settle down, see if we can fix up the shuttle and see what's what."

It wasn't a great plan, but it was the only one they had, so Ibrahim nodded in agreement. "Before we go though, lets bury this apple. Just in case the Emperor is just as much a bastard in this timeline as he is in ours. Hey, maybe we can kill him and stop the war on Carthage?"

"Hmm, let's park that idea for the moment. The consequences of these things would become very unpredictable. I mean even stopping the war on Earth is probably not wise. The more we interfere with the past, the more we put at risk the present and create an alternate future which could be worse than the one we already have. But you're right. Let's get down to that planet and get rid of this apple." *We could simply blast it with his gun and that would get rid of easily enough, but he wants to hide it so he can retrieve it later*, she thought to herself.

They soon checked over their shuttle's systems and once satisfied they could make a safe landing and departure, they flew down to the yellow planet. They saw dark black mountains forming a ridge that ran around a plateau and leaving the plateau behind they travelled north and touched down near a spike of rock that stuck out from the desert like the fingers and palm of a giant buried beneath the sand. "We will need to bury it deep," Ibrahim said as he turned to the controls of the plasma cannon and fired a steady beam of plasma down at the surface at an angle that would allow them to walk down into the hollow he intended to create.

After thirty minutes of steady continuous fire, he succeeded in boring through the sand and rock to create a deep tunnel that slipped downwards below the rocky spike. He landed the craft nearby and both he and Dr Schaffer ventured out, carrying the bag with the apple and the tablet. The tunnel Ibrahim had created was a two metre wide oval with blackened smooth walls all around and a cracked crystalline floor, where the sand had fused. The tunnel was still smoking as they made their way down into a large cavern, with red-brown rocks and boulders littering the floor and stalactites hanging from the ceiling. Ibrahim set the glass cube of the apple down on the floor in the approximate centre of the cave and began gathering rocks which he piled around it, until it was a metre high and a metre long. Dr Schaffer looked at his construction. "Hey, why don't you make it look like a grave? That way anyone who might stumble on it, might be less likely to disturb it."

"Yeah, maybe," he said as he began piling more stones alongside the mound to make it longer. At last he decided he had done enough and stood up from his work; his knees and hands covered in red-brown dust. The cairn he had built was now a metre tall and almost two metres long. He turned to Zaid's bag and pulled out the inscribed stone tablet.

"I have no idea what it says, but I think it belongs here. What do you think?"

"Sure. Why not."

He placed it gently down on the top of his cairn roughly above where he had left the apple beneath and both he and the scientist then turned and trudged their way back up to the shuttle. Once back aboard, Ibrahim lifted off and hovered a short distance away, using his shuttle's jets to keep the craft stable. Using the shuttle's plasma cannon, he fired at the base of the rocky spikes that jutted from the desert floor and the stones soon tumbled into the tunnel he had created. He then fired at the length of the tunnel, collapsing its roof and burying any sign the tunnel had existed at all. Once they were satisfied the apple was buried and there was no obvious sign of disturbance, they flew back up to orbit the unknown yellow planet. The desert wind blew sand across their burial site as they left, and Ibrahim hoped it would remain undisturbed there until he was ready to collect it again, though how he would find where he buried it, he didn't know. *At least it's hidden from the Emperor*, he thought.

He turned the shuttle towards the Hydraxian star and began manually engaging the shuttle's Alcubierre engines. *The Emperor will be arriving on Hydrax Prime soon*, he thought. *I will need to make peace with him if am to survive and work out a way back to Carthage.*

A large flake of gold paint floated down from the ceiling of the battered shuttle and came to rest on the back of his ungloved hand. For a moment he admired the gilded appearance of his skin, as an idea began to grow within him. He looked across at the body of the Alexion droid which still sat behind him in one of the seats, *I must create a new, better civilisation. One worthy of the Eroehznayn*, he thought. *I must build an Empire.*